THE DARK HORSE

and Other Stories

With a Touch of Magic

K. L. Small

Carousel Acres Publishing

Brooksville, Florida

The Dark Horse and Other Stories with a Touch of Magic

Cover photo and design by K. L. Small

Publisher: Carousel Acres Publishing

ISBN: 979-8-9900863-4-0 (paperback)

ISBN: 979-8-9900863-3-3 (e-book)

LCCN: 2025908163

First Edition December 2025

www.kathleenlsmall.com

Dedicated to Rick, my husband,
who has been with me
on this journey through life

Contents

Introduction

THIS COLLECTION CONTAINS SEVENTEEN short stories, twelve of which were previously published. Two stories were initially performed on stage as one-act plays and have been adapted into narrative form. Three other stories are released here to the public for the first time.

Each entry is followed by a section entitled "The Story Behind the Story." This feature provides background on where the story was originally published and how it was created. These extras add an explanation of what inspired the piece and other tidbits of information.

Stories have been grouped together by their general nature. For instance, the time travel stories are separated from fantasy and more supernatural tales. Some are short, while others are lengthier. Stories can be read in any order.

Enjoy! Reviews are always appreciated.

K. L. Small

December 2025

The Magic
of
Time Travel

The Dark
Horse

1860

I urged Fireball into a full gallop. The pony responded, and her hooves thundered against the dry ground. Puffs of dust exploded with each footfall. We dodged around clumps of pale gray sagebrush and raced past a herd of buffalo. With every stride, the mail pouches squeaked against the saddle leather, and the wind whistled by my ears.

Barely seventeen, short and skinny, I rode a fast horse, carrying mail across the frontier. Ten days from St. Joe to Sacramento was the goal. Fireball and I were nine miles into this morning's run to Sand Springs Station.

The pony snorted. Her nostrils flared, and her heavy breathing matched the beat of her hooves. *Getting tired.* Her exhaustion pressed into my mind.

"We're almost there. Got to keep going." I tapped my boot heels against Fireball's sides and leaned forward.

We flew over the ground, while the mare's mane whipped against my face. Dust swirled around us, and I coughed. The thrill of the ride coursed through my body. My dead parents would never have imagined their son, little Mike Barnes, riding for the Pony Express.

I spotted the stone walls of the way station in the distance and waved my hat. "Yippee!" Quickly, I lifted the bugle to my lips and blew three short bursts to warn the station master we were approaching. "He'll get my next horse ready."

Fireball tossed her head. *You should go back to the carousel.*

"You're right." I lowered the bugle and fumbled for the black cord hanging around my neck. With a tug on the cord, a brass ring emerged from my shirt. I held it in my gloved hand. The sun glinted off its smooth surface.

Once, I had made the mistake of racing into a station, jumping off Fireball, transferring the mail pouches to the saddle on a fresh horse, and riding away on the next leg of the trip. It had taken me a week to reunite with Fireball. I needed her to return to the carousel and my real-time life. I wouldn't make that mistake again.

I closed my fingers around the magic ring and imagined myself back on the carousel in Barnwell Park, Upstate New York. With a blast of cold air and a blaze of colors, I transitioned across time.

When I opened my eyes, I was astride a wooden carousel horse with a bugle carved into the saddle. Smiling, I patted the arched neck before me. "Thanks, Fireball. I enjoyed our ride."

Anytime. Her warm thoughts settled in my head.

With my wrinkled hands wrapped around the pole in front of me, I slowly lifted my leg over the horse's back and carefully lowered myself onto the carousel platform. My hips and knees ached from the effort.

My body reminded me I was seventy-two, not a youthful Pony Express rider. Heading toward the exit, I shuffled past the brightly painted ponies. Many invited me to join them for a ride. I politely declined. My old body wasn't as agile as it had been years ago.

Before leaving the carousel, I paused next to the dark horse—a plain black jumper on the second row. His eyes were wide in fright, and his mouth open, exposing his teeth and tongue. He hadn't spoken to me yet, so I didn't know his name. "You're the only one I haven't ridden."

Children scampering off the ride avoided me, eyeing me with a nervous expression. I'm sure they thought I was a crazy old man talking to a wooden horse. I suspected my family thought the same thing.

I limped over to the bench by the carousel entrance, where my redheaded grandson, Russell, slumped, his cap pulled low over his face. He always looked depressed. "Russ, my boy, you should ride with me next time. You never know what adventure awaits."

The boy rolled his eyes. "No thanks, Grandpa."

I sighed. Ever since I moved in with my daughter and her family, the relationship with my grandson had gone downhill. Giving up his bedroom for me didn't sit well with either of us, but Carla had insisted.

On the walk home, I told Russell about the challenges of being a Pony Express rider in 1860. The boy gave me a skeptical look. He didn't question me, but the doubt was there in his eyes. Like the kids on the carousel, he thinks I'm a crazy old man, too.

The next day, I sat next to the bedroom window in my rocking chair, keeping the movement slow and steady. The wooden slats creaked in a comforting way. Sweet Violet had loved this rocker, despite my complaints that it was noisy. Now, I cherished it as a reminder of my late wife, that and the handmade quilt on the bed. I recalled her working on the colorful fabric squares, stitching an intricate pattern across the patchwork top.

The hands on the face of my watch crept toward 3:30. Russell would be home from school soon. Then we would walk to the Barnwell Park carousel. Carla insisted the boy accompany me. I guess she figured the ten-year-old would ensure I didn't get lost.

At the sound of the front door opening downstairs, I hobbled over to my chest of drawers and splashed on some cologne. Violet always loved the woodsy scent. A quick check of the cord around my neck confirmed the brass ring was tucked inside my shirt. I slipped on my walking shoes and headed down to the kitchen.

Russell leaned against the kitchen countertop, munching a cookie. His shoulders drooped, and his eyes were downcast.

I frowned. Trying to lighten the mood, I asked, "How was school today?"

"Okay." He shoved the last bit of cookie in his mouth.

"Ready to go to the carousel?"

The boy shrugged, and I took that as acceptance.

At Barnwell Park, the lively music from the carousel's band organ greeted me before I could see the shingled roof of the carousel pavilion. My pace increased in anticipation of today's ride.

"Russ, my boy. Do you know how many horses are on this carousel?"

He mumbled something I couldn't hear.

"There are sixty horses in four rows, and I've ridden all but one of them."

The boy glanced at me with a raised eyebrow. "How do you know that?"

"I just do." I couldn't tell him that each horse had a distinct personality, name, and history. Or that they talked to me. Not in words that people could hear, but in my head. And they each took me for a ride into the past, thanks to the magic brass ring.

"When you ride the last one, we don't have to come anymore?" The boy sounded way too happy.

"Don't be ridiculous, Russ. I can ride them all over again." I had ridden some of them several times already. "You sure you don't want to ride today?" I always offered, and he always declined.

I hurried to join the line of riders waiting to enter the carousel's platform, excited about today's adventure. I had made a personal goal to ride every horse on the carousel. The dark horse was the last one left for me to ride, and today was the day.

When the gate opened, I touched every horse I passed, and they each greeted me with warm wishes. Some asked if I would ride them today. I gave the same answer to each of them. "Today I ride the dark horse."

With stiff joints, I mounted the dark horse, glad that he hadn't stopped in his highest position. I settled into the saddle and stroked the glossy black neck. "What's your name?"

No answer.

I looked at the smaller paint horse to the left. Patches and I got along well. Every ride on Patches took me back to days when kids wore fringed vests and cowboy hats while sitting on the paint pony to have their photo taken. The chubby pony loved standing still for the kids. "Patches, why won't he answer me?"

He says it won't end well. Patches' words sounded somber.

"What's his name?"

He has a couple. He was happiest being called Big Jim.

The carousel attendant called out, "Stay on your horse. The ride will start shortly."

I tugged on the black cord around my neck, and the brass ring emerged from my shirt. I held it in my hand and closed my fingers around its smooth surface.

The attendant rang the bell, and the band organ played a peppy march tune. The high-pitched notes spun around me. With a shudder, the carousel moved forward.

"Here we go, Big Jim." I closed my eyes in anticipation of the familiar blast of cold air and blaze of lights that meant I was traveling through time.

The carousel circled slowly and gradually increased speed. The horses rose and fell. I rode the motion, imagining Big Jim in a ground-covering gallop, but nothing happened. I was still on the carousel, going up and down. Why wasn't I transported back in time? Why wasn't Big Jim talking to me?

I opened my hand to check the ring. Was the magic used up? I thought about the possibility that I could no longer have time travel adventures on the carousel figures. In desperation, I called aloud, "Patches, is the magic done?"

Several children riding nearby horses turned to stare at me. Their eyes accused me of being a crazy old man. I'd seen that look before.

I steadied myself. *Patches, why isn't the magic working?*

The painted figure rose and fell beside me. *The magic is fine. He doesn't want you to get hurt.*

Tell him I'll be careful.

Suddenly, I sensed a solid, gentle presence in my mind. I held tight to the carousel pole in front of me and closed the fingers of my other hand over the brass ring again. The gust of wind hit me straight in the face, and bursts of colors exploded before my gaze.

When the transition was over, I was standing in a field under a bright blue sky with leather reins in my hands. Before me were two massive draft horses—a black and a gray. Between us was a plow and the broken ground, rich and fertile. I was younger, stronger, and muscular. My aches and pains of old age were gone. I didn't know what year it was, but sensed we were in the Midwest and this was a time before diesel-fueled tractors.

Big Jim snorted and leaned into the harness. The plow jerked forward, and I followed, holding tight to the plow's wooden handles. The plowshare cut into the sod, releasing an earthy smell of fresh-turned soil. I peeked at the long, straight furrow behind us.

We worked for hours, turning at the end of each row. The sun sank lower in the sky, and the dinner bell clanged. It was hard, satisfying work.

"Well done, boys," I said to the team.

Champion plow team at last year's state fair. The pride in Big Jim's words filled my head with his contentment in a good day's labor.

"Thanks for sharing this with me." I patted Big Jim's rump, then pulled the brass ring from around my neck and pictured myself back at the carousel. After the usual jump through time, I was back on the wooden horse, and the band organ music died down as the carousel stopped moving.

I had done it. I had ridden all sixty horses on this carousel and was feeling pleased with myself. "Patches, I met my goal."

Big Jim says to come back tomorrow if you're feeling brave and prepared to die. There was no missing the tremor in Patches' words.

I dismounted slowly, with my old legs complaining about the movement. As Russell and I walked home, I mulled over the possibility of dying on one of these time travel rides. Sure, there had been dangerous situations, but I never came close to dying. If I died in the past, what would happen to my family? Would my children and Russell have been born? My head pounded at the thought. Or would I be a missing old man with a silver alert reporting my last whereabouts being the carousel?

"Are you okay, Grandpa? You seem pretty quiet." The boy's face wore a worried expression. "You usually talk a lot after one of your rides."

"Sorry, Russ. I have a lot on my mind."

I didn't sleep well that night. Tossing and turning, I wondered what could take a peaceful plow horse into a life-threatening situation. Should I ride him tomorrow and find out?

The next day, Russell and I walked to the park as usual. I told him how before modern tractors, horses pulled plows to grow our crops. How they competed in fairs to prove which team plowed straighter and faster. How a hard day's work was its own reward. I continued talking to keep my mind off what might be ahead.

Once we were at the carousel, I went directly to the dark horse. "I'm here, Big Jim."

You might not come back. His tone was grim.

"You'll keep me safe."

There was no answer from the dark horse.

The carousel bell sounded, and the band organ wheezed into life. With a groan, the carousel moved forward. I grasped the brass ring in my hand and braced for the blast of cold air. A whirl of colors and sounds flashed around me.

When they stopped, the bright colors were replaced with a gray haze and misty rain. My modern clothes had changed into a drab olive-green wool coat and breeches. I recognized the shape of the helmets on the American soldiers around me. World War I, the "war to end all wars." Only it didn't.

I rode in a rudimentary saddle on Big Jim's back. In the harness beside us was another horse, but without a rider. When I looked back, two more rows of horses, with one rider per pair, pulled a two-wheeled wagon carrying three gunners, followed by a 75mm artillery piece. Somehow, I knew what everything was and what was expected. We were the American Expeditionary Forces in France.

"Private Barnes, get that horse moving!" the captain shouted. "We need this gun in place. General Black Jack Pershing says we're taking the fight to the enemy."

"Yes, sir." I urged Big Jim forward along the muddy road. His hooves disappeared into the thick muck. The mud rose to his knees.

Artillery fire exploded around us in loud, angry bursts. Clouds of acrid smoke hung in the air. These were our guns firing over us to clear the way for our doughboys to advance. Our gun had to move ahead as they made progress.

Mud sucked at the horses' legs, and Big Jim struggled to lift his front leg. His muscles strained with the effort. He pressed his shoulders into the harness with a grunt. The leather straps creaked, and the chains clanked. The wheels behind us inched forward.

"You can do it," I said as calmly as I could. My heart pounded, and I tried to breathe slowly.

With a mighty heave, Big Jim found a better foothold and surged forward. The horse beside us whinnied in panic. The hitched team battled through the mud with riders yelling and waving whips. Gradually, we pulled the gun ahead.

The rain increased, and visibility reduced to a few feet. All that mattered was one more step forward. The sucking sound of the mud and the roar of the exploding shells were constant, mixed with the screams and moans of the injured. I had heard of the horrors of war, but now I was living them. The smell of death, decay, and despair overwhelmed me. I trembled uncontrollably.

I warned you. Big Jim snorted.

We slogged on through the mud. The footing got worse, and I slid off Big Jim's back to lead him through a large puddle. Only it wasn't a puddle; it was a deep shell hole, and the bottom was somewhere well below my boots. I floundered in the water. My wool clothes weighed me down. Desperately, I swam back toward Big Jim. I had to return to the carousel. With trembling fingers, I groped for the brass ring.

A whizz whistled by me, followed by a bang. Clods of dirt and mud flew through the air. The blast hurled me across the water and hit the team of horses. Horses screamed in pain. Big Jim collapsed into the mud.

"No!" I struggled through the deep water and lifted his head from the mud.

Big Jim's nostrils flared, and a trickle of blood dripped from his mouth. *Hurry. Go back while you can.*

"I'm so sorry." Tears welled in my eyes, and I gripped the brass ring in my mud-covered hand. I imagined myself on the carousel and listened to Big Jim's death rattle.

"Mommy, why is that man crying?" the little girl sitting on Patches said, pointing at me.

"I don't know," her mother said. "But let's leave him alone." She hustled her daughter off the carousel.

I sat on the dark horse with the same empty feeling I had when my sweet Violet died. Big Jim was silent. I was a broken old man sitting on a carousel horse. I couldn't move.

"Grandpa, are you ready to go home?" Russell called from outside the carousel fencing.

Numb, I slipped off the horse and stumbled to the exit. None of my past adventures had prepared me for this. I didn't say a word to Russell on our walk home. I went straight to my room and sat in the rocking chair, mourning a painful loss.

I thought I had lost everything when my wife died. My kids had meant well, but they decided I was too old to drive or live by myself. They took my car keys and sold the little bungalow Violet and I had shared for over forty-six years. Everything was gone except the magic brass ring. Now, with Big Jim's death, I wasn't sure I wanted the ring anymore.

Several hours later, Carla turned on the light when she came into my bedroom. "Dad, are you feeling all right?"

How could I tell her I was crushed by the death of a horse in a muddy French field, in some World War I battle that happened before I was born? She would say it was dementia talking.

"Carla, could you take me to the library tomorrow?"

"Certainly, Dad. What are you looking for? Maybe I have a book that would interest you."

"I'd like to learn more about horses in World War I." I wasn't sure what I was looking for, but I had to know more about what had put Big Jim in that situation.

Carla patted me on the knee. "We can go online after dinner and see what we can find out."

My mood brightened. "I'd like that."

True to her word, after dinner, my daughter turned on the computer and typed a few words into the search. She leaned forward and read several articles. "This is pretty grim, Dad. Millions of horses died during that war. Conditions were terrible for them." She pulled up several black-and-white photos on the screen.

I had lived those images. With a sigh, I studied them closely. "What happened at the end of the war?"

She typed a few more words and scanned the screen. "Most of the horses were left behind. They were malnourished and sick." She paused. "Here's a story that has a happy ending."

I peered at the computer screen and read the article about war horses that had survived. It gave me a glimmer of hope.

The next day, I hurried back to the carousel with a plan.

Russell kept saying, "Slow down, Grandpa."

"One day, Russ, you'll ride the carousel with me." I needed to pass the magic brass ring along to another generation.

"Maybe," he said without enthusiasm.

"You'll see, but there's something I need to do today."

On the carousel, I raced to the dark horse and climbed aboard. "Big Jim, take me back to the time you came off the ship in France, before you were picked to pull the gun."

When the music started, I grasped the brass ring with excitement. In all my time travel adventures, I had never tried to change history. I always was careful not to interfere with anything historically significant. But today, I was determined to save Big Jim's life.

After the transition, I found myself at the remount depot with hundreds of horses milling around. The stockyard smell filled my nostrils. Amid the mass of animals, Big Jim towered over the smaller horses.

A British officer marched over to me, his uniform clean and crisp. He sported a thin mustache over his upper lip.

I saluted properly and stood at attention.

"Private, my horse was shot out from under me last week. The doctor cleared me to ride again, but I need a new mount."

I smiled. "Sir, I have a champion horse for you. He's smart, steady, and a hard worker."

"Sounds like a winner. Let's see this chap."

I paraded Big Jim before the officer. "He's as sound as they come."

The officer nodded. "Not my usual hunt horse. Looks more like a plow horse."

"He's calm under fire. He'll stand still for you, even in extreme conditions."

The officer walked around Big Jim. "I'll need a different saddle, but he'll work."

"Sir, I have one request."

"Speak up, lad." The officer stroked his mustache.

"When you return to England. Please take this horse back with you. He deserves to have a peaceful end."

"Bloody right. We all do."

"Your promise, sir." I was overstepping my position, but I had to try.

"My word as a gentleman. If I survive, he'll have a home with me. Now, cheerio!" The officer took Big Jim's lead rope and walked away. The horse followed obediently.

Big Jim glanced back at me. *Thank you.*

In a minute, I realized my mistake. The same mistake I had made with Fireball. I needed to be with Big Jim to return to the carousel. I might not see him again, the way I did with Fireball. I'd be trapped here in 1918.

I raced through the crowd of soldiers and horses. Finally, I spotted Big Jim's rump ahead and reached out to grab his tail. Quickly, I pulled the brass ring from around my neck and wished myself back on the carousel.

A blast of air and a wild swirl of colors rushed before my eyes. When the transition was done, I sat on the carousel horse as the music faded and the ride slowed. Several strands of Big Jim's tail hair dangled from my hand. I had changed his history!

I never rode the dark horse again. I hated to find out whether he and the British officer made it back to England. In my life—what's left of it—I will forever dream of Big Jim running in a green field, free from harnesses and far from the memories of war. Perhaps when my life is over and I'm reunited with Violet, we'll ride the dark horse, his big hooves thudding against the sod, and his mane streaming before us. Together forever.

Originally published in *The Accidental Time Travelers Collective*, Volume 1, 2022.

The Story Behind the Story for "The Dark Horse"

After I finished writing the manuscript that ultimately became *The Magic Carousel*, I was querying agents, participating in pitch events, and promoting the story on social media. One thing I did was respond to daily posting prompts about time travel. Since my carousel novel included time travel, it was a great opportunity to interact with other time travel authors.

Soon, a group of twelve authors banded together to create a short story collection called *The Accidental Time Travelers Collective*. My writing had focused on middle grade novels, so I needed an adult story for the anthology. In *The Magic Carousel*, the grandfather gives his grandson a magic brass ring that allows time travel when riding a carousel. I realized the grandfather might be the main character I was looking for, and he could travel back in time to a situation that I never would use for my middle grade character.

My grandfather was in the U. S. artillery during World War I. He kept a diary of his time in France, and I read all his entries. Additional research into the conditions he faced, and the role of horses during the war increased my understanding of the difficulties and challenges. The story of "The Dark Horse" became clear.

The photo on the cover of this book was one I took in Syracuse, New York, during a National Carousel Association annual conference. The expression on the horse's face reflected the attitude I imaged for Big Jim.

In October 2023, the Florida Writers Association presented a Royal Palm Literary Award Gold Award to "The Dark Horse" as a published short story.

Lake Lorelei

THE EXULTANT POWER COMPANY helicopter swept low over the muddy water, the roar of its blades sending a pair of finches into the sky. As the aircraft flew by, the brightly colored fall leaves rippled in the trees along the flooded river. From the backseat, Elizabeth peered out the window at the houses surrounded by water, vehicles abandoned along the submerged roadways, and a collapsed bridge. The remains of a building floated down the overflowing waterway. Using her phone, she took several photos of the damage.

She spotted emergency responders in boats traveling from house to house. Her throat tightened. The dam failure had been so sudden, there was no chance to warn residents to evacuate. She closed her eyes and willed away the tears that threatened to fall.

After taking a deep breath, she returned to watching the rescue efforts. Last year's dam failure risk report had projected higher property losses and potential deaths because of increased development downstream from the dam. But what she was looking at wasn't a computer simulation. It was a real disaster.

"I hear the CEO has to brief the Board about this mess." Carl's voice crackled in her headset.

She faced the Emergency Response Director seated beside her and replied, "He wants the initial assessment by 4 o'clock today. My operations staff are already at the plant."

"We'll have to step up inspections at all the dams," Carl said. "Can't have this happen again."

"No. Never again…"

The pilot's transmission cut into their conversation. "Just heard the confirmed death count is ten. Probably will be higher when the search is completed."

"Shit." Carl slammed his hand onto his leg.

Elizabeth cringed. Her tears welled again, but she fought them back.

"CEO is going to be pissed. He'll fire someone's ass over this." Carl narrowed his eyes at her.

"I've only been in charge of the Division for a month."

"It won't matter. He's got to pin this on someone. If you don't want it to be you, then find someone to offer up as the fall guy."

"As the Director of Hydro, I'm here to find out what happened, not blame one of my employees, unless someone deserves it." She glanced at her watch and wrote "October 21, 2023" in her notebook. Quickly, she jotted her observations, then pushed the button on her headset to talk to the pilot. "Let's get a closer look at the dam."

The helicopter banked slowly around the dam's spillway. As they hovered over the structure that once held back Lake Lorelei, she studied the intact concrete and took several photos. Beside the dam, she focused on the wide gap in the earthen berm. The river had carved a new path through the eroded opening.

"The embankment breached," she said, scribbling several more observations in her notebook.

Lake Lorelei was gone now. The lower water level exposed the bare sides of the empty impoundment. Ten feet above the water's surface, the dark mouth of the tunnel that used to carry water to the hydroelectric power plant yawned on the rocky slope.

"We should land soon," Carl said to the pilot, "to drop off Elizabeth. Then, you can take me to the local emergency command center."

"Roger," the pilot responded.

Elizabeth held her hand to her stomach, trying to quiet the nausea. The extent of the damage and her anxiety about briefing the CEO were the chief causes, but the fuel fumes were not helping.

The helicopter rose over the mountain and descended toward the power plant site, roughly following the path the tunnel took through the mountain. On her first visit to the plant, the regional manager had told her it was a mile long, as the bird flies. The tunnel had been filled then, carrying water from Lake Lorelei to power the turbine blades in the power plant below.

As the plant came into sight, Elizabeth sighed at the amount of debris covering the switchyard. Two transmission towers tilted at a crazy angle. The rampaging water had done significant damage here too. After capturing several more images, she slipped the phone into her back pocket.

The pilot slowed their descent and landed in a small clearing beyond the switchyard. "Watch your step getting out and stay clear of the tail rotor," he said. "I'll be back to get you at 15:00."

Elizabeth removed her headset, placed the notebook in her field kit, and grabbed her hard hat. As she stepped out of the helicopter, her steel-toed boots sank into the mud. Her foot slid in the slick muck, and she grabbed the helicopter door to keep from falling. The strap of her field kit swung off her shoulder, and the bag banged into her back. Wobbling, she managed to keep from falling. Mud splashed across the bottom of her khaki pants.

Slipping and sliding, Elizabeth moved away from the rotor's downwash. A sucking sound accompanied each step she took. She settled the hard hat on her head, slung the field bag over her shoulder again, and straightened the collar of her corporate polo shirt with its Exultant Power logo.

Inside the power plant, she met Hank, the operations supervisor. Elizabeth gave him an overview of what she had seen from the helicopter, studying his concerned reaction to her words. "Hank, tell me what happened here."

"This morning, Lorelei was operating well. All three units were humming at full power. She was working like a champ. The skies were sunny and clear. Water level in the lake was below the spillway. Everything was normal. But at 9:24 a.m., the operator noticed the turbines running rough." Hank shook his head. "You can't see the dam from the plant, but when the operator checked the remote videos, he saw the water level dropping in the lake, and he went outside. A wall of water was overtopping the riverbanks. He called me immediately. I told him to shut the units down and call 911 to report the flooding."

Elizabeth nodded. "Good reaction."

"Water hammer could ruin everything." Hank pushed his hard hat forward and rubbed the back of his head. "I came right over. By the time I got here, the river had flooded... everything."

She heard the catch in his voice. "Is your family in the flooded area?"

"We live the next county over. The operator lives in the mountains, so we're not affected. But, the thought of the loss..."

Relieved that their families were safe, her thoughts returned to the upcoming CEO briefing. "Any chance it was sabotage?"

"Doubt it, but the Security Department is reviewing the plant videos."

"How old is the dam?"

Hank rubbed his chin before answering. "Let me think. Went into operation in 1923." He paused. "Why, the old girl is one hundred years old."

Touched by his affection for the plant, she jotted details into her notebook. "Tomorrow, we'll have a team of specialized consultants onsite to do a detailed analysis of the dam."

The operations supervisor frowned. "I can tell you what happened. From what I saw on the security cameras, the embankment gave way. Don't need a bunch of outsiders crawling all over the place."

"It will add credibility to our report to have independent experts give their opinion. Have you checked the penstock for damage?" She noticed the startled look on his face. He probably thought the new female director didn't know anything about hydro plants.

"Been focused on the turbines and generators."

"Understandable," she said. "While you investigate possible damage to the units, I'll check for exterior problems."

Once she was outside, she glanced at her watch and slung the field kit over her shoulder. On her own, she hiked uphill alongside the pipe that carried water to the plant. She stopped at the spot where it connected with the tunnel to Lake Lorelei. To her surprise, the penstock had separated from the tunnel. She examined the rusted bolts that should fasten the pipe to the concrete around the tunnel opening. The vibration from the sudden drop in water level must have fractured the bolts.

Planning to take a picture of the damage, she reached for her phone, but it was missing. Frantically, she rummaged through her field bag. She remembered using it in the helicopter to photograph the flood damage and putting it in her back pocket. She must have dropped it during her precarious moments getting out of the helicopter.

She reached into her field bag and removed a flashlight. With a click, the beam of light blazed on high. She peered into the dark opening, moving the light along the rough rock walls, slick with moisture. Several loud splashes sounded repeatedly. She focused the flashlight in the direction of the sound. Could someone have been sucked into the tunnel as the water level dropped?

"Anyone in here?" Her voice reverberated in the darkened space. The splashing continued.

The gap between the penstock and tunnel was wide enough for her to squeeze in. All her safety training told her not to enter by herself, but Hank knew she was outside. She dropped her field bag to the ground. After taking a deep breath, she slid through the opening. Inside, the damp air smelled like a fish market.

The footing of the rock surface was irregular and slippery. Elizabeth put her hand on the rough wall to steady herself. She flashed her light from one side of the tunnel to the other.

"Is anyone here?" Her words repeated deep into the darkness and faded without an answer.

Keeping a hand on the rock surface, she inched forward. Her light caught a ripple in the middle of the uneven floor. She drew closer and centered the beam on the puddle of water. Her heart beat faster. A fish fin broke the surface and sent droplets flying. She relaxed. "Sorry, buddy. That's all you have now."

Elizabeth looked back at the small sliver of light that marked where she had entered, then continued walking up the tunnel. With each step, the air grew denser. Her arms and legs moved in slow motion, like going through water. She stopped at the sting of static electricity. Then, her flashlight flickered. Worried, she turned around and headed back toward the opening. Her footsteps echoed through the tunnel. The light dimmed and barely lit the way. "How could I be so foolish?"

Elizabeth's boot slipped out from under her, and she fell. Her hard hat tumbled off, and her head slammed against the rock floor.

Elizabeth lay still, breathing through the pain. The sound of dripping water thundered in her brain and competed with the throbbing of her temples. After a few minutes, she opened her eyes to blackness and panicked. Then, she recalled venturing into the tunnel and the thrashing fish. She groaned and rolled over. With a deep breath, she sat up and waited for the dizziness to pass. Her fingers probed the sore spot on the side of her head. At least there wasn't any blood.

Groping around the rough floor, Elizabeth searched for the flashlight but found nothing.

Damn.

She struggled to her feet and rested her hand against the rock wall. With unsteady fingers, she reached for the phone in her pocket, but recalled it was missing

Her jaw tightened, and her head throbbed.

She remembered her watch had a light and felt her wrist, but it was gone too. She checked further up her arm.

The pounding in her head slowed her thoughts. She touched her arm again and fingered the long sleeve that covered it. Her short-sleeved company shirt was gone.

Her hands dropped to her pants. The fit and fabric felt different too. Her heart raced. None of this made sense.

With her fingers creeping along the damp wall, she inched forward one step at a time, heading downward, toward the plant. She froze at the muddled sound of voices ahead of her. A wave of relief surged through her.

"Hello," she shouted. "Hank, I'm here."

Metal clanged against rock repeatedly. The noise didn't sound like the actions of a search party.

"Hello," she called again. "I need a light." Shouting made her headache worse.

The clanging stopped, and an unintelligible voice came from ahead of her. A steady tap of footsteps reverberated through the tunnel. A tiny point of light moved in her direction. She increased her pace, heading toward the light.

"Over here. Keep coming." Her voice shook with nervous energy and anxiety.

The light shone in Elizabeth's eyes. Slowly, she recognized it was a flickering flame, not a flashlight. She blinked and tried to make out the face of the man who held the lantern. In the irregular light, she couldn't clearly see his features, but he wore a woolen cap instead of a hardhat. And, why wasn't he using a flashlight? It wasn't Hank.

"Who are you?" the man demanded.

"I'm Elizabeth Gilroy." With her rescuer standing in front of her, the throbbing of her head increased. The dizziness returned, and she moistened her lips. "Director of Hydro—"

"Ain't supposed to be anyone in here. How'd you get in?" The man came closer and held the lantern higher. A trickle of sweat ran down the side of his dirt-covered face.

Jumbled thoughts rolled through her mind. "I must get to a phone. It's important."

"Ain't no phone round here." He grabbed her arm.

Her annoyance growing, she shook free of his grip. "You can't treat me like this. I'm the Director of the Division. You work for me."

The man laughed in her face. "Sure y'are, and I'm Thomas Edison. Now, how did you get in my tunnel? Mr. Wilson'll hear about this."

Her rattled brain fumbled through the Division's management team. No one named Wilson came to mind. Her attention shifted to the lantern, and she pointed at it. "Why are you using that rather than a flashlight?"

The man pushed the cap further back on his head, exposing a hank of black hair. "Look baby, you don't know from nothing. You ain't got a light, and you're beefing about mine."

His words confused her further, while her legs trembled and threatened to give out. She felt woozy, and her vision blurred. "Hit my head... not feeling well." She wobbled and sank to the ground.

Vaguely, she sensed herself being lifted and carried out of the tunnel. The man's sweaty odor was the last thing she remembered.

Angry voices roused her to consciousness. Before she opened her eyes, she listened to their dispute while she lay still on a narrow cot.

"That's outrageous, Roy," a gravelly voice said.

"Ain't no telling what he done wrong. Plain and simple, he fell putting up the last forms for the dam."

Elizabeth recognized the second voice. It belonged to the guy in the tunnel with the lantern.

"We can't keep losing workers like this." Pacing footsteps followed.

"Mr. Wilson, ain't uncommon for men to get hurt and killed on construction jobs."

"That is not acceptable. Not on a Wilson Enterprises job." The response was accented with a loud noise that sounded like a fist pounding on wood.

"Shhh. You'll wake her up." The voice was female and young.

Elizabeth stopped pretending to be asleep and sat up. Her eyes roved around the small room. Two hurricane oil lamps brightened the space. A cluttered wooden desk filled the middle of the small room.

Two men, one in a fedora and the other wearing a cap, faced each other. Elizabeth recognized the man with the cap—Roy. The sweat-stained sleeves of his shirt were rolled up. Mr. Wilson was older, heavier, and wore a three-piece tweed suit with a bow tie and fedora. The people and the room looked like they could be from an old-time movie. Elizabeth's mind spun.

"See. You woke her up." The young lady in a low-waisted dress jumped up from a chair by the desk and came over to the cot. Her hair was gathered away from her face with two pink bows. "Sorry, miss. How do you feel?"

"I'm confused," Elizabeth said, locking eyes with the teen.

"Mr. Miller said you hit your head."

Her hand went to the side of her face. "Mr. Miller?"

"Roy. He found you in the tunnel." The teen's eyes darted to the younger man, and she blushed.

Elizabeth recognized the lovesick look, but a glance at the girl's dress set Elizabeth's nerves on edge. The old-fashioned dress belonged at a costume party.

"My name's Lorelei Wilson. What's yours?"

In shock, Elizabeth stared at the teen. Lorelei? Just like Lake Lorelei?

"Did you hear me?" the teen asked. "What's your name?"

"Sorry. I'm Elizabeth Gilroy."

Mr. Wilson came over to stand beside Lorelei. Eyeglasses with small round lens perched on the tip of his nose. "I want to know what you're doing here."

I hit my head when I fell, Elizabeth thought. Maybe I'm imagining all this.

She blinked and licked her lips.

"I expect an answer." Mr. Wilson leaned closer to her. The chain of his pocket watch swung away from his vest pocket.

She hesitated. "I'm an engineer."

Mr. Wilson snorted. "There are no women engineers."

"Papa, she seems different. Maybe she studied in a big city or in Europe."

"That's not likely." Mr. Wilson scowled at Elizabeth. "Why are you here? How did you get here?"

Her gaze shifting from Lorelei to Mr. Wilson, Elizabeth steadied her thoughts. "I came to investigate the dam's failure. I must report to the CEO in a few hours."

The heavy-set man harrumphed. "You can tell those investors who sent you to spy on me that this dam is not a failure. It's almost finished and will be generating electricity soon."

What's he talking about? How can the dam not be finished yet? Unless...

"What's today's date?" Elizabeth asked, desperate to know.

"October 21," Lorelei replied.

"What year?" The sound of her racing heart pounded in her ears.

The girl gave her a strange look. "Well, 1923, of course."

Elizabeth closed her eyes and let the wave of nausea pass.

Is it possible I've gone back in time?

She rubbed her forehead, questioning the crazy idea.

I hit my head. Maybe I have a concussion.

"Madam," Mr. Wilson said in a stern voice. "You still haven't told me what you're doing here."

"Papa, can't you see she's not feeling well?" Lorelei hurried across the room and returned with a tin cup of water.

Roy took off his cap and ran his hand through his dark hair. "She was almost down at the end of the tunnel. Damn near coulda killed her with the last blast."

"You're lucky to be alive," Mr. Wilson said. "I don't want to add Miss Beth Gilroy to the list of deaths."

"Papa, it's Elizabeth. Not Beth," Lorelei said.

Elizabeth sipped the water and tried to sort out what was going on.

How could it be 1923? I can't be a hundred years in the past.

"Too many good men have already died on this project." Mr. Wilson paced around the room. He pulled out his pocket watch and grunted.

"Boss, I need to get back to the tunnel. Gotta finish the blast. Then, we'll hook up the pipe. Can start raising the water level now. We'll be running in no time at all."

Elizabeth heard the words, but they didn't make sense. Her befuddled brain sorted through the normal start-up procedures. "Wait, before you connect the penstock, you have to flush water through the tunnel."

Mr. Wilson glared at her. "What do you know about building a hydroelectric plant?"

Much more than you can imagine.

"The tunneling debris needs to be cleaned out before you send any water into the turbines. Otherwise, you'll ruin the blades."

Roy nodded. "Boss, she's right. Ain't no way to get rid of all the rock chips in there. Bet water flowing through will do the job."

"I hadn't thought about that." Mr. Wilson ran his index finger along his upper lip. He stepped closer to Elizabeth. With a softer tone, he asked, "Any other suggestions?"

Sitting on the cot, Elizabeth suppressed a grin. "Don't open the valves to the turbines until the water level in the lake is several feet over the mouth of the tunnel."

Roy and Mr. Wilson looked at each other and then back at her. Their facial expressions changed from doubtful to intrigued.

"The water level in the lake will drop quickly when the plant starts pulling water," she continued. "You want to make sure there's sufficient water to prevent problems." Hank's words came back to her. "Water hammer could ruin everything."

"Good advice," Mr. Wilson said. "Thank you. Although I still don't know why you're here. If you think of anything else, please let me know." Turning to Roy, he nodded. "Get to it."

Settling the cap on his head, Roy headed toward the door. He winked at Lorelei.

"Be careful," Lorelei said. Her cheeks turned the same color as the pink ribbons in her hair.

With Roy gone, Mr. Wilson returned to his desk. He shuffled through several papers, then rested his head in his hands. "Too many deaths," he muttered to himself.

Lorelei perched on the edge of the cot beside Elizabeth. "You sound like you know about construction. Would you like to see the dam?"

"I sure would." Despite her headache, she jumped up. Seeing the dam under construction was an amazing opportunity she couldn't resist.

If it's still under construction, then this really must be 1923. Maybe I can learn if something during construction caused the dam to fail.

"Papa, we're going to walk around."

Mr. Wilson frowned. "I agreed you could come if you stayed in the office. It's dangerous out there."

"Oh, Papa," Lorelei said with a giggle. "Stop treating me like a child. I'm sixteen now."

Mr. Wilson rose from his seat. "That's why I'm going with you."

Outside, Elizabeth stood still and scanned the work site. Workers bustled around the riverbanks, collecting rubble and loading it in wagons pulled by horses. A black Model T truck sat near the construction office. Any doubts she had about it being 1923 disappeared. Even from a distance, she noticed the lack of modern equipment, hard hats, and gloves.

"Are you coming?" Mr. Wilson called over his shoulder.

The reality of her situation sinking in, Elizabeth followed him. On the way to the scaffolding around the dam, they passed a small shed.

"What's in here?" she asked.

"Gunpowder and fuses used to blast the tunnel through the mountain," Mr. Wilson said.

Elizabeth gestured toward the building's door. "There should be warning signs posted."

A man with suspenders paused by the shed and puffed on a cigarette.

"Put that out," Elizabeth commanded. She pointed at the lit end of his cigarette. "You can't smoke this close to explosives."

The man scowled at her and grumbled, "They get the right to vote and get all uppity."

"Get rid of it." Mr. Wilson advanced toward the man. "We've had far too many accidents on this site."

The man dropped the cigarette and ground it into the dirt with his boot. "Sorry, boss." Then, he walked away.

Elizabeth sighed.

I must get back to my time. This one is appalling.

"I want to see the dam embankment," she said.

Mr. Wilson's eyes narrowed. "Why?"

Think quickly.

"I heard you say that there have been deaths on this project."

"Too many."

"When it's completed, this dam and embankment will hold back a significant volume of water. If they fail, a wall of water will come racing downstream and kill people."

Mr. Wilson tugged on his vest and pulled out his pocket watch. "That's a big if."

"Papa, let's show her what she wants to see." Lorelei took Elizabeth's arm and pulled her forward.

After glancing at his pocket watch again, Mr. Wilson said, "I've got to get back to the office. You two can get a closer look, but stay away from the river. The current is wicked strong after that storm yesterday."

"Of course, Papa."

Heading toward the dam, they walked alongside the cofferdam that diverted the river around the work site. The water rushed by in a roar. Elizabeth stopped to stare at workers on scaffolding as they smoothed concrete along the top of the dam's spillway.

No safety harnesses or tie-offs. No wonder there have been deaths.

But more horrendous was the placement of dead tree limbs and trunks with the soil to form the embankment.

"They can't do that." She stared at the tree debris.

"Can't do what?" Lorelei looked puzzled.

"The embankment will fail if the compaction isn't uniform. Those tree branches and chunks of roots will decompose and create voids."

"I don't know what you're talking about, but you should tell Papa."

They hurried back toward the construction office, running past the cofferdam. "I know a shortcut," Lorelei called over her shoulder. She turned off the worn path to the office and ran closer to the riverbank.

"Be careful." Elizabeth's warning was lost in the thunder of the rushing river.

On a rough patch of ground, Lorelei slipped and tumbled down the steep bank into the water. She splashed wildly in the swirling current. Heavy with water, her dress sank and pulled the teen under. A minute later, her head rose above the surface. She gulped a mouthful of air before being pulled under again.

Elizabeth dove into the water and swam toward Lorelei. The water churned around her. With each stroke, she drew closer to the floundering girl being carried away by the river.

"Help!" Lorelei's head bobbed above the water briefly, then disappeared. She surfaced for a moment and sank again.

Desperate, Elizabeth swam in the girl's direction. She reached out to grab Lorelei's arm when the girl struggled to the surface, but a tree branch tumbling in the river crashed into Elizabeth's back. Her body twisted around, and she lost sight of Lorelei. Pushing free of the branch, Elizabeth dove underwater to search.

For a moment, she spotted the girl's long dress ballooning in the water. She grabbed a handful of fabric and pulled. Gasping for air, Elizabeth rose to the surface with Lorelei's limp body. Using a side stroke, Elizabeth angled them toward the cofferdam. With awkward motions, she pulled Lorelei to the water's edge.

Workers leaned over and dragged the still body of the teen up the bank. One worker ran to get Mr. Wilson, while another helped Elizabeth up the cofferdam's steep slope.

When she reached the top of the berm, Elizabeth bent over Lorelei and checked for signs of breathing. Finding none, she quickly tilted Lorelei's head back and began mouth-to-mouth resuscitation. She listened for a heartbeat.

"Come on, breathe." Recalling her CPR training, she positioned her hands over Lorelei's chest and pressed hard.

Huffing for breath, Mr. Wilson ran over and dropped to his knees by his daughter. "What are you doing to her?"

Elizabeth continued the chest compressions. She breathed into Lorelei's mouth. This time, water gushed out of the girl's mouth. As Lorelei sputtered and coughed, Elizabeth turned the girl on her side. "You're going to be okay. Breathe slowly."

Lorelei's eyes opened. She sobbed in loud gasps.

Mr. Wilson took off his jacket and laid it over his daughter. He stroked her wet hair. "I told you to be careful." Looking over Lorelei's head at Elizabeth, he said, "I don't know how you did it, Miss Beth, but I owe you a big thank you."

"We should take her inside where she can get dry and warm up," Elizabeth said. A shiver ran through her body.

And, it wouldn't hurt me to warm up too.

Once they were back in the construction office, and the fire in the stove was blazing, Elizabeth sat beside Lorelei on the cot.

We both could have drowned. If I died here—in the past—my family would never know.

The complication of living in two different times was unsettling.

I need to get back to my time.

"I'm never going in the water again," Lorelei wailed.

Patiently, Elizabeth took the teen's hand. "One day, when the dam is done and the water level has been raised, there will be a beautiful lake here. It will be a peaceful place for boating. Fish and waterfowl will live here too."

"That sounds wonderful, Beth," Mr. Wilson said.

Lorelei stopped crying and sniffled. Her father handed her a handkerchief.

"We shall call it Lake Lorelei," he said with pride.

"Really, Papa?"

He nodded. "Of course."

"Lake Lorelei will power the hydroelectric plant too," Elizabeth said.

"Now we're talking." Mr. Wilson smiled. "That calls for a drink."

"But Papa, that's illegal."

Elizabeth searched her knowledge of the 1920s.

It must be Prohibition.

"I have my sources," Mr. Wilson said in a low voice.

He set a bottle of amber liquid on the desk and retrieved two glasses from a desk drawer.

"Where's mine?" Lorelei asked.

"In a few years." He poured a generous amount in one glass and a smaller amount in the other. He handed the smaller portion to Elizabeth.

She sniffed the contents and took a sip. It brought tears to her eyes and warmed her insides immediately. Several sips later, she was feeling relaxed and determined to tell Mr. Wilson what she thought of his project. But, before she could say anything, the office door burst open and a filthy Roy bounded in.

"We blasted through the last of the rock. We're through." Roy grabbed Lorelei and twirled her around the room.

"That's worth drinking to." Mr. Wilson found another glass and splashed the moonshine into it. He handed the glass to Roy and raised his own. "To the completion of the tunnel."

Elizabeth stared into her glass.

Now that it goes all the way through the mountain, can I return to my time by going back through the tunnel?

Roy downed his drink and set the glass on the desk with a solid thud. "We need to finish the embankment so we can raise the water level and clean the debris out of the tunnel."

Mr. Wilson nodded. "Better hurry. Winter temperatures will freeze the water soon."

"I'll get right on it, boss." Roy headed to the door.

"Wait." Elizabeth put her hand out to stop him. "That embankment must be redone."

"What?" Mr. Wilson stomped over to stand in front of her.

"That embankment isn't acceptable. There are tree branches, roots, and other debris in it. It will never compact enough to meet standards."

Roy frowned. "Ain't no standards."

She closed her eyes at the memory of the flooding that followed the dam failure. When she opened them, she fixed both men with a stern glare. "You're going to kill people downstream when that embankment collapses."

"Ain't nobody downstream," Roy said.

"There will be." Elizabeth pointed in the general direction of the dam. "You're building a power plant, so there'll be electricity for people. That means there will be development." She struggled to control her emotions. "When the dam fails..." She caught herself. "If the dam fails, the water from Lake Lorelei will rush downstream, and people will die."

"Papa, we can't let that happen," Lorelei said.

Mr. Wilson looked from his daughter to Elizabeth. "Roy, check that only good, clean fill is used on the embankment."

"And, there should be rocks placed along the upstream side of the embankment to protect it from waves blown across the lake."

"But, boss. It's almost finished—"

"Do it."

Silently, Elizabeth celebrated her victory. These changes might prevent the embankment from eroding and save the lives of those downstream.

Now, I must get back to my time. The way back must be in the tunnel.

"You should take Lorelei to the doctor, just to be sure her lungs are clear," Elizabeth said.

Mr. Wilson nodded. "Good idea." He pushed his glasses higher up on his nose. "Can't be too careful with my Lorelei."

"Oh, Papa."

"Let's go." He motioned for Elizabeth to join them.

"I'll stay here," she lied. "I'd like to rest for a while."

This might be my only chance to get back to the tunnel.

Mr. Wilson gave her a questioning look. "I'll be back in an hour or two."

After they were gone, Elizabeth sneaked into the upper end of the tunnel. As she eased down the slope, she raised a lantern to light her way. The flickering flame cast an irregular light across the hewn rock. She hoped each step brought her closer to going home, to returning to her own time.

Ten minutes later, the air became thick, like she was moving through a dense fog. Her skin tingled with tiny shocks of static electricity.

This is what it felt like before.

Determined, she struggled forward against the resistance. With each slow movement, she gasped for air, her lungs burning. She fought through waves of dizziness and focused on one step at a time. Sparks of light flashed before her eyes.

With a final lunge against the invisible force, she was through. Her heart pounded, and she took a deep breath, freed from the band of pressure across her chest. Suddenly, the lantern was gone, but a ray of light glowed ahead. The end of the tunnel.

She hurried down the rest of the passage, eager to learn if she had returned to her real time.

What if it's a totally different time?

Stepping through the gap between the tunnel and the penstock, she stopped and stared.

Below, a fleet of television vans were parked beside a large white tent. Even from a distance, she spotted Hank being interviewed by a reporter. She sighed in relief.

But the pieces didn't add up. When did the tent get put up? What day was it? Elizabeth walked down the slope and headed to the tent. Was it the same day as the dam failure or some other day? She took a few more steps.

As Elizabeth approached the tent, she stopped to listen to Hank's interview.

"Lorelei Hydroelectric Power Plant has been in service for one hundred years," he said. "This centennial celebration is a milestone for us. We're upgrading the plant equipment and replacing aged pieces like the pipe that carries water from Lake Lorelei to the plant."

Elizabeth frowned.

Centennial celebration? Why wasn't he talking about the dam failure? There weren't any plans to update the plant equipment.

"And, here's the Director of the Hydro Division. She's the one you should be talking with today." Hank gestured for Elizabeth to come over and join the reporters.

Tentatively, Elizabeth stepped forward. Her head was spinning with the adjustment from 1923 and the uncertainty of what was going on now.

A big banner hung from the tent, proclaiming, "Lorelei Hydro-electric Plant 1923-2023." She looked from Hank to the reporter.

Everyone is smiling. They aren't upset about the dam failure.

With sudden realization, her heart almost skipped a beat.

There wasn't a dam failure. No lives lost.

A reporter asked, "What would you like our viewers to know about this place?"

Elizabeth grinned. "The lake and the plant are named for a young lady named Lorelei. She was the daughter of Mr. Wilson of Wilson Enterprises. He and a dedicated team of workers braved dangerous work conditions to build the dam and the plant." She continued talking for five minutes about the construction effort.

Hank announced, "We have a special presentation in the tent from a guest who's almost as old as the plant."

Hank led Elizabeth and the reporters into the tent. A stand at the front of the tent displayed a bronze plaque, and next to it was an elderly lady in a wheelchair.

"I'm Sybil Jessup, president emerita of the local historic museum. Lake Lorelei was named in honor of my mother. I'm the granddaughter of the man who had the vision to undertake this project, and daughter of Roy and Lorelei Miller." The elderly lady lifted her hand toward the display stand. "We discovered the original dedication plaque in the museum's store room and felt it belonged here at the plant. This sign memorializes the names and roles of the people who built the dam and power plant one hundred years ago."

Elizabeth blinked back happy tears at the thought that Lorelei and Roy had married, and this old woman was their daughter.

"My mother often told me," Sybil said, "she almost died during the construction of the dam, but she owed her life to a very special person, whose name is on the plaque. Because of that person, my mother went to college and became an engineer, the first female engineer in her graduating class."

With the memory of Lorelei's rescue running through her head, Elizabeth read the inscriptions on the memorial and smiled at the experiences she had shared with each person. Her eyes fixed on the last line. She read it aloud, "Special thanks to Beth Gilroy."

Hank leaned close to Elizabeth. "A relative of yours?"

Wiping a tear from her eye, she laughed. "Maybe."

Originally published in *The Accidental Time Travelers Collective*, Volume 2, 2023.

The Story Behind the Story for "Lake Lorelei"

The success of Volume 1 of *The Accidental Time Travelers Collective* (see The Story Behind the Story for "The Dark Horse") led to the decision to create Volume 2. Rather than writing another carousel story, I tapped into my professional background in the energy business. "Lake Lorelei" emerged as a fictional account tied to my years of working on hydroelectric projects in upstate New York.

As required by law, dam failure studies were performed to identify areas that would be impacted by a dam failure. Such events would be catastrophic and offered a dramatic opening for the story. Having flown in several helicopters, I knew they were often used to assess damage after disasters.

One hydroelectric construction project I worked on included dewatering an existing tunnel used to carry water to the turbines. In my imagination, that tunnel became the conduit for time travel back to the 1920s, a time when many dams were constructed.

Writing coaches recommend you write what you know. This story was a wonderful way to draw upon knowledge and experiences I gained while employed.

Box 13

I RECEIVED THE FIRST contact from my future self when I was in kindergarten.

On a warm April afternoon when I was six, a plain manila envelope came to my home in the mail. It bore my name in large block letters. I never got mail, so this was quite exciting for me, but concerning for my mother. Mom handed me the envelope with a worried expression on her face. "Who would send you mail?"

With a shrug, I seized the envelope and ripped it open, exposing a crayon drawing on green construction paper.

"What is it?" She peered over my shoulder.

I pulled out the paper and studied the stick figures. My name was printed under the figure in the middle of the page, with Mom and Dad beside me. A fourth smaller stick figure held Mom's hand.

"Did you draw this?" she asked.

"No. I drew a bird in a tree today."

She took the drawing and envelope from me and examined both, turning the drawing over several times. "No return address," she said, almost to herself. "No note."

"Who is that?" I pointed at the tiniest stick figure with a curl of red hair.

Her hand went to her belly, and she blinked quickly. "We were waiting to tell you. We're having a baby girl later this year. You're going to be a big sister."

That news caught me by surprise, and I had a hundred questions. I forgot about the drawing, but later that evening, when I was getting ready for bed, Mom and Dad discussed it in hushed voices.

In the morning, the drawing hung on the refrigerator door. I wondered who sent it but had more pressing things to think about, like what should I wear to school and what snack would we have in class.

My little sister, Emily, joined our family in October. She was a happy baby with a few strands of red hair that I loved to shape into a curl at the top of her head.

A year went by until I received another envelope addressed to me. This time, the drawing was a bit more refined, with names neatly printed under each person. It included a black-and-white dog named Patches.

Mom frowned. "We don't have a dog. I wish I knew who was sending these drawings. It's kind of scary."

"It's not scary. It's fun." I enjoyed getting mail. How many seven-year-old kids got anonymous drawings sent to them? It made me feel special.

When Dad came home from work, he carried a box into the house. "Come see what I found under my car."

Mom and I gathered around the box, startled when a puppy poked its head out of the open flaps. One ear was white, the other black.

"Patches!" I danced around, then reached for the puppy.

"Oh, no." With her hands on her hips, Mom glared at Dad.

"It'll be good for the girls," he said. "They'll learn responsibility."

She retrieved the drawing that had come in the mail and showed it to him. "We received this today. How did someone know you were bringing home a dog?"

Patches licked my face and wagged his tail. I didn't care who sent the drawing, but I was glad it included my new friend.

The following year, on my birthday, I received another anonymous envelope. This time, the drawing included a note written in simple words I could read. The picture showed me riding a yellow two-wheel bicycle with blue streamers attached to the handlebars.

"Am I getting a new bicycle?" I asked, jumping up and down. "The paper says, 'Always wear your helmet.' I must be getting a bicycle."

My parents glanced at each other. Their eyes wide, and eyebrows raised.

"Go look in the garage," Dad shrugged and stepped out of my way.

I hurried there and spotted a brand-new yellow bicycle with blue streamers, just like in the drawing. Whoever was sending me these pictures knew what was about to happen. I had to find out who was mailing the envelopes. When I went back inside, Mom and Dad were arguing.

"You're sending these to her," she yelled at him.

"I'm not. Let me see the postmark on that envelope."

"Should we notify the police?" She sounded terrified.

"Mom, don't worry," I said. "These drawings are great."

"How can anyone know all these things?"

"I don't know," Dad replied. "But no sense calling the police. There's no postmark and no stamps. Besides, nothing bad has happened."

I was relieved he calmed Mom's concerns. Me, I wasn't worried. I could hardly wait for the next envelope.

Over the years, many more envelopes arrived. As I got older, the drawings were replaced with typed letters signed simply: "Me." I grew increasingly curious who it was that sent me tips on what musical instrument to play, what club to join in high school, or where to apply for a part-time job. Even after we moved to a new city, the letters continued to find me. It made me feel very special and intrigued. The post office couldn't tell me where the envelopes came from, and there were no clues in the letters either. It was a mystery—a mystery I wanted to solve.

When I turned eighteen, the letters changed. For the first time, the mysterious writer asked me to do something. I read the typed letter twice. It told me to wrap my favorite book in plastic, take it to the nearby park, and bury it behind the veteran's monument. The request puzzled me.

Why does the letter writer want me to do something so pointless?
I did it anyway.

When no one was around, I dug a hole with a garden shovel, making it deep enough to hide the carefully wrapped book. Hastily, I shoveled the dirt back in place and tamped it down, hoping the park attendant wouldn't notice the bare spot at the monument.

The next day, a letter arrived, thanking me for the Anne McCaffrey book and noting all the things that I liked best about it. Unnerved, I put the letter down and paced around my bedroom. How did the author of the letter know I dreamed of being a dragon rider of Pern? I never told anyone about that.

The timing of the response was baffling. I just buried the book yesterday. Not time enough for someone to dig it up and write a letter, so I received it today. That wasn't possible. Maybe Mom had been right to be nervous about these mailings.

I returned to the park with my garden shovel and examined the spot behind the monument. Nothing had changed. When the area was clear of parkgoers, I got down on my hands and knees to dig. As soon as my shovel hit the bundle, I rocked back on my heels. The book was still there. At the sound of footsteps approaching the monument, I hurried to replace the dirt. Brushing the soil off my hands, I wondered how the letter writer had known what I buried. For the first time, I was worried.

The answer came the next day in the mail. My hands shook as I read the two-page letter. When I flipped to the second page and glanced at the signature, I dropped the paper. It fluttered to the floor, and I backed away. I recognized the signature, the flourish under the name and the way the i was dotted. The signature was mine.

With trembling fingers, I retrieved the letter and sat on my bed. After taking a deep breath, I read the contents again.

Dear Caroline,

For twelve years, I have been mailing you messages. It's time to tell you who I am.

I am you *in the future. You are* me *in the past. Hard as that may be to understand, we are the same person. I knew you were going to have a baby sister and get a puppy because I grew up with Emily and Patches. I loved riding that yellow bicycle with Patches running alongside.*

Quite by accident, I discovered a "time mailbox" while I was working at the post office. Box 13 was unique, and no one wanted to use it. Rumors and superstitions were tied to the box. I spoke with a lot of old postal workers and retirees about it and discovered—according to them—I could send mail back in time. All I had to do was put the date when I wanted the letter delivered and the address, of course. It didn't need a stamp.

The first mailings were simple drawings, then advanced to letters and suggestions based on my memories. I worried about whether I was interfering with my personal history, but it was fun to think I was in touch with my younger self.

I have no memories of ever receiving mysterious letters while I was growing up, so perhaps this whole venture was a waste of time. While my letters disappeared when I put them in Box 13, I had no way of knowing if they were getting to you. So, I decided to try opening a more active exchange.

When I wrote asking you to bury the book, it was a way to test if it was possible for you to get things to me. I figured a monument in the park was not likely to be moved, which made it a safe place to bury the book. It worked. I was able to unearth it, a little worse for being buried all that time, but still readable.

I know communication from the future must be overwhelming. It certainly has taken me years to think through whether I should do this. I hope you understand that I've never wanted to change the past in any way. That's the stuff of science fiction movies. I'll never send you winning lottery numbers or stock tips.

However, I have another request of you. Go to your local post office, the one on Main Street, and get PO Box 1313. Nobody ever wants that number. You can leave me messages in the box, and I'll get them in the future. No need to put a stamp on them. I know this must sound confusing, but it should work. In your time, the messages will pile up, and it will seem like no one is getting them. But in your future, I'll retrieve all your messages from the box and respond quickly.

Yours, as always,

Caroline (future Me)

How was this possible? Yet, every message had been correct or worked out exactly as presented. I closed my eyes and rubbed my temples. Thinking about the idea of time traveling messages was hurting my brain.

The next day, I went to the post office and paid for the specific PO box. With the key in my hand, I asked the postal worker, "Is there a Box 13 here?"

He blinked quickly and stammered, "Never heard of it."

I walked away with a half-smile.

He knows, but he's not telling me.

At my box, I made sure the key worked. It was empty. I had crafted the wording of the first note to my future self carefully. I scanned it again. "What year did I dig up the book?" I slipped the message inside the box and locked the door.

My answer arrived the next day in the mail. I struggled to imagine life in 2071 and quickly did the math. I would be sixty-six years old. But more surprising was a second envelope without a stamp and post-mark. I opened it and found a small, silver sphere; shiny, like a polished ball bearing. The note that came with it was brief.

Use the enclosed holobook in a holotechpro.

I scratched my head.

What in the world is a holobook?

A hasty computer search didn't give me an answer. The metal ball had no markings. I rolled the smooth surface between my fingers. Quickly, I jotted a question to my future self, asking what it was, and took the note to my PO box.

The answer that came a day later shocked me. Following an apology, my future self wrote:

I must have written the wrong year on the envelope. The holobook technology won't exist for another twenty years or so, in your life. I'll convert the manuscript to the written format used in your timeframe.

Even though I wasn't a techy kind of person, I realized I had been given a glimpse into the future of books.

But why is future me sending me a manuscript?

Several days later, I received a flash drive in the mail, along with a brief letter. I read it twice.

This will be my last communication. The post office where Box 13 is located is scheduled to be demolished tomorrow, since people no longer mail letters. With Box 13 gone, I won't be able to send you anything. This flash drive is my final gift to you. I debated whether to send it, but wanted you to know all will be well. Be sure to get a job at the post office.

No more letters from the future?

The thought made me teary-eyed. My future self knew me like no one else. I would miss getting her—my—letters. They had been part of my life since kindergarten. Then another thought hit me.

If I don't get a postal job and find Box 13, there will never be letters sent. But I must have gotten the job, because there were letters. Has my future already been determined? What happens if I don't go to work at the post office?

In a daze, I carried the flash drive to my computer. When I opened the file, I discovered a novel about life in 2071. I read in amazement the technological and societal changes and conflicts that were ahead. I pondered what to do with this information.

While I considered the future of the file, I applied for a mail carrier position and was hired. Within weeks, the old timers were showing me the secrets of postal work. It was easy to encourage them to share their thoughts on the mythical Box 13. It didn't take long for me to uncover that it was protected from public access, but no one shared where it was located.

As for the file on the thumb drive, I knew there was only one thing I could do. I published it for science fiction readers and futurists. The book became a national bestseller, hailed as a sci-fi masterpiece. I became a much-requested speaker at conventions and made a fortune from book sales and speaking engagements.

"Caroline, you're a successful author. Why are you still working at the post office?" interviewers and fans often asked me.

I smiled but never admitted I still was searching for the location of Box 13. I knew I would find it one day. My future self had told me so.

Originally published in *The Accidental Time Travelers Collective*, Volume 3, 2024.

The Story Behind the Story for "Box 13"

When Volume 3 of *The Accidental Time Travelers Collective* was proposed, I hesitated. Did I have another time travel story to share? Since I was working on a women's fiction called *Letters from Shadow Oaks,* the idea of using letters to transport messages through time was my answer to that question.

I had also started doing colored pencil drawings at the time. That gave me a fun opening to introduce art as an early form of communication.

This story presented the dilemma of a time travel paradox. I leave it to the reader to decide if sending messages back to an earlier self causes a problem by altering the past or creating a time loop. My head hurt while I tried to address this. Good luck in figuring out the time travel puzzle.

The Magic
of
Fantasy

Memory Lane Park

I confirmed the details on the amusement park admission ticket. Flipping over the crisp, white paper, I read the small print, "Admittance to Memory Lane Park requires forfeiture of one memory." I took a deep breath. *Losing one memory is what I want. Maybe then the nightmares will stop.*

In the graying evening, the lights around the walled park entrance blinked in red, yellow, and green, like a traffic signal. My lips formed the words on the sign, "Memory Lane Park." The letters glowed in purple neon with an irregular humming and buzzing. Arched double doors below the sign blocked entry to the park.

Muffled carnival music and children's laughter filtered through the doors. The hint of hot buttered popcorn filled the air. My mouth watered, and I licked my lips. With the ticket in my hand, I stepped to the park's entrance. The massive wooden doors were aged, each with an iron knocker shaped like an elephant head. I grasped the elephant's trunk and tapped. The door swung inward with a groan of worn hinges.

Bright calliope music and unrestrained laughter exploded like fireworks. The aroma of cinnamon buns and funnel cakes floated by, and a sudden gust pushed me forward. After I entered, the heavy doors closed with a bang.

"Welcome to Memory Lane Park," a female voice behind me said. "I'm the Keeper of Memories."

I twirled around, but nobody was there. With trembling fingers, I held up my ticket. "I'm supposed to be here now." With a sizzle, the ticket vanished. I stared at my empty hand, shaken and surprised. *No! I need the ticket. How else can I forget that dreadful day?*

"Pick a ride, any ride, but only one," she said. "Some will add or change a memory. A few will erase a memory. One will remove all memories. Choose wisely."

The voice reminded me of my first-grade teacher. Despite my advanced age, I was a child again in a classroom full of students, desperate for the owner of the voice to listen to me. "For my entry, I want to pay with a specific memory." I had tried everything to remove the details of the event that had ruined my life—hypnosis, pills, alcohol, therapy. *This is my last chance.*

The voice swirled around me. "You don't select the memory. I do."

"But. . ." I stammered.

"Move along."

Lights flicked on beside a brick-paved pathway. I walked along the lighted pavement, marveling at each ride's illumination. Metal gears clanked into motion, and the air vibrated with the laughter, cheers, and screams of unseen park-goers.

On my right, a carousel played lively music while the solitary horse on the platform rose and fell. Each time the horse passed me, it changed colors from white to black to red. A sign at the carousel read, "The Joys of Childhood." A fragment of a memory tickled my brain. My father ran beside me while I rode my brand new two-wheeled bicycle. I laughed and shouted, "Go faster!" The image faded, but the happiness of that memory lingered.

To the left, a single boat bobbed in a water-filled canal, poised to enter the Tunnel of Love. The boat was narrow, wide enough for one passenger. The tunnel mouth loomed dark and foreboding. *I've had little luck with love. Just broken relationships and divorce.* I kept moving.

A crooked walkway beyond the carousel led to the House of Horrors. Twinkling lights decorated a sign with the message, "Face your fears with smiles or tears." *Can I smile at a fear?* I wrinkled my nose at the scent of charred wood and gasoline seeping from the entrance. A blood-curdling scream made me back away and return to the main brick path.

At the end of the pavement, a gigantic Ferris wheel towered over the amusement park. *I've never seen one this big, but there's only one gondola.* The wheel's top disappeared into the night sky and its bottom dipped into a trench below ground level. I watched the large structure spin and followed the gondola's movement up toward the stars and down into the dark pit. On the gondola's side were the words, "Highs and lows of life."

The voice—like a mosquito—buzzed in my ear, "Which shall it be? Choose carefully."

I looked back at the rides I had passed, but my heart drew me to the Ferris wheel. *I want to forget the lowest point of my life.* I made my decision.

The enormous wheel slowed, and the gondola's door swung open. I stepped into the metal car and sat on the vinyl-covered seat. The door slammed shut with a clang, and the Ferris wheel glided into motion. I rose skyward. Below, the city lights glowed, and I spotted the road that I refused to travel on since the accident.

The gondola rocked slightly, and a cool breeze brushed my face. The wheel rotated slowly, taking me higher into the dark sky, where the moon and stars shimmered. At the top of the ride, I remembered eating warm Christmas cookies at Grandma's house. The sugar melted in my mouth, and the smell of baking brownies filled her cozy kitchen. I was six again and so happy.

The wheel continued moving, and the gondola descended into the pit. Blackness surrounded me, and my gut tightened. The squealing brakes and screech of tires gave way to my children's screams. Then it was silent, dark, painful. Alone with my family's death, I bore the responsibility. *I was driving. It was my fault.* "Take this memory away!"

The Ferris wheel picked up speed, and the gondola rocketed skyward again. At the zenith of the arc, I remembered the pride of my high school graduation, followed in the pit by the memory of my job termination and a deep sense of loss. The wheel spun faster. The joy of marriage, then the bitterness of divorce. Births. Deaths. Accomplishments. Failures. My head throbbed as the memories clashed.

The stars and city lights blurred. We circled repeatedly. I clung to the gondola's metal frame as the car swung wildly. Flashes of memories blasted through my brain. Then there was only oblivion.

When I regained consciousness, the gondola door was open. *My mind's blank. No memories. Nothing to recall.* My heart pounded hard against my chest; my thoughts a tangle of confusion. *Yet there's a peacefulness about having no memories. I'm free from my past.*

The Keeper's voice interrupted my musing. "You chose the ride that erased all your memories. So, you take my place now. When visitors arrive, greet them and decide which one of their memories will become yours." The voice faded away.

An icy shot of park instructions and procedures burst into my head. A chill coursed through my veins with an understanding of my new role.

Then a metallic knock at the entrance reverberated through the park, and the doors swung open. Clutching a ticket, a bewildered man entered. Invisible, I floated beside him.

"Welcome to Memory Lane Park," I said. With a thrill, I seized the ticket and scanned his memories for one I wanted to own. "I'm the Keeper of Memories."

Originally published in *Thrills and Chills*, Florida Writers Association Collection 14, 2022.

The Story Behind the Story for "Memory Lane Park"

"Memory Lane Park" was published in *Thrills and Chills*, the 2022 anthology of the Florida's Writers Association. It was selected #1 in the collection.

When the theme of the 2022 collection was announced as thrills and chills, I didn't think I could write a story that would fit the theme. After all, I don't read horror books or watch horror movies.

At the time, I was enrolled in David Farland's online writing class. The first assignment was to write a description of a setting from a character's perspective. I wrote about an unusual amusement park that operated on taking or giving memories. That assignment became the short story I submitted for the collection. I was shocked when it was selected as the top story in the collection.

Help Wanted

BRIANNA SHOVED HER HANDS in her jeans pockets and trudged down the back alley toward her small studio apartment. She kicked a dilapidated cardboard box that blocked her path. With a squeal, a gray rat scurried down the alley.

"That's right. Run away!" The words tore at her heart. Returning to Iowa felt like running away from her dream of success on Broadway. But what else could she do? She was unemployed and behind in her rent.

She passed the back door of the tattoo parlor, then glanced at the grimy window of the narrow shop next-door that faced the alley. Its nondescript entrance was easy to overlook. The smudged lettering on the window read "Mydori's Mending." Why hadn't she noticed this shop before?

Brianna smirked. Who mended clothes these days? Her jeans had shredded knees, and she would never dream of patching them. Looking closer at the dirty glass, she noticed a small sign behind the window: Help Wanted - Inquire if you Dare. More curious than concerned, she reached for the door handle. The door swung open with a groan. A tiny bell jingled, announcing her arrival.

"Come in," a female voice called from the back.

After entering the dimly lit shop, Brianna closed the door. The bell tinkled again, and the sounds from outside faded. Lavender and sandalwood scents mingled in the air. She closed her eyes and inhaled deeply. This would be a pleasant place to work, and so close to where she lived.

"I'm here about the job." Brianna raised her voice for the person who had yet to come into the room. She glanced around the tiny shop. Spools of thread were mounted on a display stand. A row of glass jars with buttons sorted by color lined a shelf. Several garments lay on a waist-high countertop. No sign of ribbons, laces, or bolts of fabric. A single empty chair sat near the dingy window.

"Very good." The thump of a cane against the floor and shuffling footsteps grew louder. An older woman barely five feet tall emerged from the back room. She wore a plain blue skirt and a white top with an embroidered neckline. A gray tabby cat trailed behind her.

"Are you the owner?" Brianna asked.

"I'm Mydori. Can you sew on a button?"

Feeling confident, Brianna smiled. "My grandmother taught me to sew. I worked as a stitcher for the costumer on Broadway." She lowered head. "Until the show closed."

Mydori clumped across the floor to the chair by the window.

"I can patch a tear and darn a sock," Briana continued.

"Useless skills." As Mydori settled in the wooden chair, she shook her head. "No one wants darned sock. Buttons. They want buttons. That's all I do."

Brianna narrowed her eyes. What kind of mending shop only did buttons? "I can handle buttons and buttonholes."

Mydori waved an arm toward the button jars. "Show me."

Brianna approached the jars with buttons in assorted sizes and shapes. Her fingers brushed the glass of the first jar with red and burgundy buttons. Warmth crept up her arm. Then she slid her hand to the container of green buttons with metal shanks. The taste of green mint made her open her mouth in surprise. At the smell of cut grass, she backed away from the jar.

Quickly, she glanced at the old woman. Mydori's head was bowed, her eyes closed. The old woman's gnarled hands shook with an irregular tremor. The cat sprawled on Mydori's lap; feline eyes fixed on Brianna.

She needed this job. The alternative was going back home to the small-town life she had escaped. Taking a deep breath, she grabbed a jar with wooden buttons. She removed the glass lid and reached in for the toggle button that caught her attention. When her fingers closed around it, she gasped. She stood in a dense forest with trees surrounding her. Branches shifted in the light breeze. A shaft of sunlight fell across her face.

"That will do nicely," Mydori said.

The trees disappeared, and Brianna stood trembling with the toggle button in her hand. "What happened?"

Mydori fished a packet of needles and a spool of brown thread from a basket by her chair. With crooked fingers, she offered them to Brianna. "Sew that button to the jacket on the counter."

With a nod, Brianna took the needles and thread. She picked up the jacket and spotted where a button was missing. She stared in shock at the remaining buttons, all wooden toggle buttons. They matched the one she held. Exactly!

Despite her shock, Brianna threaded the needle and sewed the button in place. As she stitched, the tension in her shoulders eased. She imagined herself in the woods with leaves rustling and birds singing. Peacefulness settled over her, and she hummed until she tied the final knot.

"All done." Brianna handed the jacket to Mydori.

The old woman stroked the button and nodded. "You're hired."

"Don't you want to know my name or have me fill out a form?"

Mydori leaned forward and rose slowly. "I know what I need to know."

"Okay," Brianna said tentatively. "How much do I get paid? What are my hours?"

Shuffling to the counter, the old woman reached into a metal box and removed a yellowed envelope. She handed it to Brianna without speaking.

After opening the envelope, Brianna's eyes widened. She leafed through the bundle of cash. There was enough to pay her back rent and most of next month's expenses.

"I appreciate this," Brianna stammered, "but it's too much for sewing on one button."

"Brianna, you did much more than that."

Brianna nearly choked. "You know my name."

"Of course. I've been waiting for you."

"I don't understand." Brianna rubbed her sweaty palms against her jeans.

"You will... in time." Mydori snorted. "After I teach you the secret."

Brianna swallowed and ran her tongue over her lips. She glanced at the envelope in her hand. What had she gotten herself into? The sign had warned if you dare.

"A secret?"

Mydori smiled at her. "I need to pass along my knowledge. My days of Cinderella gowns are over." She wiped a tear from her eye. "That was a mighty fine garment. But my fingers can barely hold a needle now. You're my new apprentice. I'll teach you about buttons."

Brianna furrowed her brow. "Buttons?"

"And other things." Mydori's laughter sounded like a cackle. The old woman nodded. "People pay dearly for my buttons. They're infused with magic. The right button will change the life of whoever wears it. And you have the gift."

"What gift?" Brianna recalled the warmth from the red button jar, the unexpected taste of mint, the smell of grass, and the forest experience. Could that be the gift?

"Another secret. More tomorrow." Mydori hobbled into the back room.

"I'll be back. You can count on that." Empowered, Brianna tightened her hold on the envelope. She removed the Help Wanted sign from the window and left the shop. No running back home to Iowa. She would be a success in New York City after all, once she learned the rest of Mydori's secrets.

Originally published in *Secrets*, Florida Writers Association Collection 15, 2023.

The Story Behind the Story for "Help Wanted"

"Help Wanted" appeared in the 2023 Florida Writers Association collection titled *Secrets*. It was selected #8 in the collection.

The character Mydori in this story first appeared in *A Dress To Remember: A Fairy Tale* as a mysterious dressmaker. I liked her magical seamstress skills and decided to bring her to a contemporary urban setting but reduced her magic to sewing on enchanted buttons.

Masterpiece

With her pulse thumping, Delaney hesitated before gingerly pressing her age-spotted hand against the art studio's busted door. It swung open, groaning on broken hinges. She gasped.

Paper littered the floor. The drawers of her art supply cabinet lay empty in a chaotic pile beside her overturned drafting table. A puddle spread from toppled water containers.

Her eyes darted to the display wall where her finished painting should be. Gone.

Her hand flew to her mouth.

Footsteps echoed in the hallway behind her. She spun around, afraid the thief had returned. In relief, she recognized her business manager sauntering toward her.

"Good morning, Delaney." A broad smile lit his face. "I'm here to pick up your portrait for the Legacy Exhibition."

"Andrew." Her voice quivered. "The studio was robbed. The painting's gone."

He peered into the studio and frowned. "Have you called the police?"

Delaney shook her head. "I just got here."

She stepped past the damaged door, shuddering at the violation of her creative space. Despite her arthritis, she bent down and righted the water containers.

She blinked back tears. "Why would someone do this?"

"Money. You're a successful artist. The stolen pieces will wind up on the black market. What did they get?"

"At least a dozen unframed paintings." Delaney gestured at the shelf barren of her artwork. She exhaled slowly. "And the self-portrait for the exhibition."

"Thank goodness most of your collection is already there."

Delaney balled her hands into fists. "I worked so hard on that self-portrait."

"Do you have another one? Something at home?"

She glared at him. "I hate self-portraits. I only did it because the Legacy demanded one."

Andrew stroked his chin. "You used to do them, years ago, before you took up your dark architectural style."

"No one wants a watercolor of an old hag." She stooped stiffly to pick up sheets of paper from the floor.

"Delaney," Andrew scolded. "I wish you saw the beautiful, creative person the rest of the world sees."

With a snicker, she brushed a strand of white hair away from her eyes. "Maybe long ago."

Andrew shrugged. "But right now, I need a painting of you."

"It's too late to start over," Delaney said. "Much too late."

"The exhibition contract requires a self-portrait. There's a steep penalty for failure to perform." His eyes were apologetic. "You better start painting."

Delaney clenched her teeth and balled her hands into fists. "My paints and brushes are gone."

"Get new ones. I'll be back tomorrow." Andrew carefully stepped over the spilled water and left.

After the police had come and gone, Delaney tried to restore order to the studio. While she cleaned, she worried about how to recreate a painting that had taken her two weeks to complete. It couldn't be done without paints and brushes. She had no choice, though. While a contractor replaced the door, Delaney went shopping.

Shay's House of Fine Art Supplies stood a few blocks from her studio. The owner's knowledge of quality paints, papers, and brushes was the reason she had rented in the area. The familiar set of bells over the door jangled gaily, announcing her arrival. The aroma of solvents and paints filled the space. Racks of canvasses and sketchpads lined one wall, and bins of paint brushes stood ahead of her.

"Shay, I need your help," she called anxiously and shuffled to the counter. The hurried pace to get to the shop had left her winded.

"He's not here," a young man at the cash register said. "He had a family emergency."

Delaney leaned against the countertop and caught her breath. "I'm sorry to hear that, but I need supplies."

"I'll be glad to find them for you."

"Shay usually has my supplies set aside."

"Good," he said. "What's the name and I'll check."

"Delaney."

His eyes widened. "You're the famous Delaney? Shay talks about you all the time." He smiled shyly. "I teased him that he must be in love with the beautiful Delaney."

With her cheeks warming, she shook her head. "His eyesight is worse than I thought. He must not be able to see all the white hair and wrinkles."

He laughed nervously. "Shay told me you get anything you need."

The young man rummaged through boxes and tins behind the counter. "I found it." He placed a cardboard box bearing her name and a leather case on the counter.

She opened the box to expose a dozen tubes of watercolor paint, more vibrant colors than she usually employed. She opened the leather case and stared at the paintbrush's silver bristles. As she stroked them, her heart beat faster and a tingle ran through her fingertips.

"This isn't the brush I use."

"It was on top of the box." The young man shrugged. "You can leave it if you don't want it."

Delaney weighed her option. "I need a brush, and if Shay saved it for me, I'll take it."

Back at her studio, Delaney examined the handmade paintbrush. As she grasped the wooden handle, vibrations pulsed through her fingertips. The feeling frightened but intrigued her.

She squeezed the watercolor paints on her palette and added water, swirling the mixtures together with her new brush. Rich aromas rose from the paints. She inhaled and lowered her brush into the familiar gray puddle of paint she used in her somber urban scenes. The bristles filled with the dull color. She swiped the brush across the paper and delighted in the way it slid across the surface.

When she returned to the palette for more paint, a sensation shot up her arm, and the brush moved straight to the red paint. She fought the motion, but the brush pulled straight to the pool of paint. With a full brush, red ribbons of color splashed across her paper, accompanied by the swish of satin fabric. A long billowing dress appeared in the painting.

As night darkened the studio, Delaney turned on lights and examined her incomplete artwork. The vivid colors and freedom of the image—so unlike her usual style—made her smile. A surge of energy flooded through her. Her arthritis pain melted away. A stray piece of hair fell across her face; no longer white, but auburn.

Next, the brush raced to the green paint, and she smelled evergreens. Trees spread across the painting's background in a splash of intense colors. For hours, the colors exploded across the watercolor paper. A passion for painting filled every cell of her body.

As sunrise brightened the studio, the brush dipped into flesh tones, and Delaney felt herself pulled into the paper. She closed her eyes and let the feeling carry her into the scene with the paintbrush in her hand. The red dress swirled around her legs, and the tree branches swept across her cheek.

In the afternoon, Andrew knocked on the new studio door.

"I'm here for the painting," he called. When there was no answer, he tried the knob, and the door swung open.

He stepped inside the workspace, determined to collect Delaney's self-portrait for the exhibition. Surprised not to see the artist, his gaze fixed on the display wall. Stepping closer, he marveled at the painting of a youthful Delaney wearing a flaming red dress, dancing in a forest. Locks of auburn hair floated around her glowing face. Her eyes glittered with laughter, and she smiled directly at him. An involuntary whistle escaped his lips.

"It's a masterpiece!"

In awe, he stepped back and bumped into a work table. He reached out to steady himself, and his hand brushed against a leather packet with an image of a paintbrush on one side. He stared at the label and read it aloud. "Made from unicorn hair."

Andrew opened the leather case, but it was empty. He glanced at the painting again and noticed a silver-haired paintbrush in Delaney's hand.

With his suspicion growing, he moved closer to the portrait. The red dress fluttered as if ruffled by a breeze. Delaney winked at him and raised a hand in farewell.

Originally published in *Metamorphosis*, Florida Writers Association Collection 16, 2024.

The Story Behind the Story for "Masterpiece"

"Masterpiece" was included in *Metamophosis*, the 2024 collection produced by the Florida Writers Association to showcase member writings. With a theme that focused on change, my story envisioned a touch of magic to change the artist into the work of art.

I enjoy watercolor painting and understand how the properties of the paintbrush affect the painting experience. Better watercolor paint brushes are often made from animal fur. A brush made with unicorn hair offered that touch of magic.

The Gift

WIN, HEAD TEACHER AT the Institute for the Magically Gifted, fidgeted on the wooden stool. She watched a fat, tri-colored cat jump from the Director's cluttered table. She tapped her foot impatiently on the stone floor and cleared her throat once again.

"Master Garlot," she repeated forcefully, looking directly at the old wizard seated across from her at the table. She wondered if a little magic could improve the Director's hearing.

He nodded and snatched a lizard as it hurried across the open scroll spread before him on the table. He glanced up and scowled. "Oh, Win. It's you."

The deep lines around the wizard's mouth eased into a smile. He snapped his fingers and the lizard wriggling in his hand became a rose.

"For my favorite teacher," he said, offering it to her.

Win reached for it, but the flower disappeared. The old wizard laughed until his thin beard shook from chin to shin.

Some things never change, Win fumed. Ever since her earliest days at the Institute, she disliked being in the Director's office. Win stared warily at the wizard as he wiped a tear of amusement from his eye.

"Master Garlot, I intend to resign at the end of this session of classes." She folded her hands in her lap and sat motionless.

The steady ticking of the mantle clock and the sound of Garlot's cat scratching the table leg filled the room.

Garlot rose from his great chair and walked across the room to an oak chest. "You're just tired, dear Win." He rummaged through the various containers atop the chest's lid. "You enjoy teaching, and you're so good at bringing out the best in each child."

"I've lost interest. The years and the children are all blurred together. It's time—"

"It's time for a change," Garlot interrupted. "It's time for a fresh challenge."

He lifted the heavy lid, and a collection of bottles and tins fell to the floor with a crash. The scent of lavender and pine spread through the room.

Win breathed deeply, and her muscles relaxed. Slowly, she replied, "I would rather just leave."

The old wizard reached into the chest and removed a small red pouch. He shuffled back to his chair and cleared a space on the table, pushing aside the scroll.

"Every child that comes to the Institute has a special gift, a magical talent that is given at birth. Our task is to help them shape that skill as they grow. And you are especially good at expanding each student's magical potential."

He loosened the drawstring of the pouch and emptied the contents onto the table. A half dozen gold marbles rolled across the wood surface. Garlot examined the round baubles closely. He selected one and rolled it between his fingers.

"Usually, it is clear to everyone from the beginning exactly what magic a child possesses." He continued rubbing the gold orb. It gleamed in a shaft of sunlight leaking through the nearest stained glass window. "But a child has come to us—the daughter of a Master Enchantress and a Third Level Sorcerer. She should have a significant magical gift." He polished the glistening marble against his silk robe.

Win sighed. She knew it would be like this. "Master Garlot, please understand." She focused on Garlot's gray eyes. "I'm tired of teaching magic control and disciplining those who use their magic for mischief. I can't listen to another recitation of the Code of Magic Rights and Responsibilities. Not even one more time. I want to leave."

"This child," Garlot continued, "shows no magical talent at all." He blew lightly on the dazzling ball as he moved around the table toward Win. "I thought that with your ability to identify a child's magical gift..." He placed the warm, throbbing orb in Win's right hand and folded her fingers around it. "Perhaps you can help."

"No!"

Win knocked the stool over as she jumped up, but Garlot had snapped his finger already. She felt a surge of magic charge the air as she looked down at the empty palm of her right hand. The intricately carved door to the office swung open silently. In the doorway stood a frail girl, barely over six-years old, with a gold sash draped across her shoulders. The child stepped tentatively into Garlot's office.

Win remembered her initial visit to the Institute many years ago as a youngster. She recalled meeting the ancient Director for the first time, and how she had worried that her magic might not be strong enough to earn her a place in the exclusive school of magical arts. Her heart went out now to the child, edging closer to the wizard's table. A child with no clear sign of magic.

Yet, Win sensed a tingle of her own magic. Perhaps the girl had some small trace of magical skills that, with patience and practice, could grow and mature. Win had helped many children develop their magical talents over her years as a teacher at the Institute. Maybe she could find a tiny spark of magic in this little girl.

Win's heart raced. The magic was there—definitely there. She felt it growing stronger with every step the child took. She reached out and clasped the little girl's hands. Win trembled, and a tear ran down her cheek. She kneeled before the child, hugging her.

The little girl giggled with delight.

Win remembered all the children she had taught. She recalled their laughter and excitement as they mastered a new use of their magic. She felt the happiness and joy repeated each year with every group of students. Each jubilant face danced before her eyes. She experienced again their pride—and hers—at every accomplishment.

"Well," Garlot demanded. "What is it?"

Win picked up the child and turned toward the old wizard. "Her magic..." she said, pausing for breath, "her magic is for me."

She smiled at Garlot, gazing at him through tear-filled eyes. "Her magic is to revive memories from the past."

Then she carried the little girl toward the open door. Softly, she whispered to the child, "First, I will help you discover what fun magic can be."

The sound of Win's footsteps echoed down the hallway of the Institute long after she left the office.

Garlot chuckled as he scooped up the five gold marbles remaining on the table and returned them to the small pouch. "A good teacher is worth a little magic," he told the cat as she rubbed against his leg.

Originally published in *Beyond the Moon*, Winter Issue 1994/1995.

The Story Behind the Story for "The Gift"

"The Gift" was published in *Beyond The Moon*, Winter 1994/1995 issue. I had paid a $5.00 fee to enter the publication's fantasy contest. When the publication arrived in a manila envelope, I opened it to discover my story had won third place. I jumped up and down in delight. Then I found the $20.00 prize check that had fallen to the floor, which was even more exciting. This was my first financial success as a published author.

While "The Gift" included a school for magically gifted students, it was written years before the Harry Potter series, which debuted in 1997. Any resemblance to Hogwarts School of Witchcraft and Wizardry and Headmaster Dumbledore is a surprising coincidence.

I made a few edits from the original version because I've learned so much about stronger writing in the thirty years since it was originally published.

Em's Shop of Magical Wonders

EMERY CRINGED AT THE cobweb-covered sign hanging above the weathered green door. The faded gray letters read, "Em's Shop of Magical Wonders." Shocked to have received the business as an inheritance, she never anticipated its dilapidated condition. Aunt Emily had always spoken about it so fondly.

Determined to see the interior before the realtor arrived, Emery jiggled the antique skeleton key in the lock and pushed against the door. It swung open with a creak, and she gasped.

The drab, worn exterior had not prepared her for the explosion of color, scents, and sounds inside the shop. The aroma of cinnamon, ginger, and mint wafted through the air. Her gaze traveled from a shelf of shiny black top hats, pointy purple witch hats, brown derbies, and feathered fascinators to an umbrella stand full of canes and walking sticks in beige and walnut. Pink parasols hung from the ceiling. Woven baskets held red apples, orange pumpkins, and golden pears. White doves cooed from a coop, while a pink bunny nose wiggled through the screen of a hutch.

Emery had expected the store to feature basic magician supplies like disappearing ink and card tricks, not this odd assortment of items. She walked around the jam-packed room, stepping around larger items and pausing to examine smaller objects. She turned at a rustling sound behind her.

"Welcome to Em's," a parrot squawked from its perch.

With a smile, she approached the bird. "You must be Aunt Emily's pet." She noticed the cup filled with bird seeds. "Looks like someone's been feeding you. I wonder who."

"Welcome to Em's." The parrot flapped its wings in a blur of blue and yellow feathers.

"You need a home now that Aunt Emily's gone, but you can't stay at my apartment."

A rapid series of taps at the door announced an arrival.

"That's the realtor," Emery said to the parrot, then headed to the door. Swinging it open, she looked down and blinked in surprise.

A short, bearded figure, almost as wide as tall, waddled into the shop. His brown robe brushed against her as he entered. "Here for the dragon's tooth."

"What?"

"The tooth. The dragon's tooth. Emily said she would have it for me."

Emery cleaned her throat. "I'm sorry. She passed away. The business is closed."

Stroking his wiry beard, the visitor pursed his lips. "She promised."

Emery hesitated, unsure who she was speaking with, and how he could believe he would get a dragon tooth here. Dragons weren't real.

He placed his short arms on his stout hips. "Waiting."

Flustered, Emery pointed at the door. "The shop is closed. I don't know anything about what my aunt promised. The realtor is coming to list the building for sale."

"Sell? No." His eyebrows drew together as one hairy mass.

The parrot squawked and flew from its perch to the shop's cluttered countertop. With its orange beak, the bird pecked at a tin box near a ledger. "Welcome to Em's."

Emery hurried to the box and opened it. A yellowed fang rested on a wad of cotton. She extended the box toward the bearded figure.

He took the tooth and removed a leather pouch from his pocket. The contents clanked together. "Payment."

Shaking her head, she said, "I can't take anything for that. I'm not running the business."

He tossed the bag on the countertop with a thud. "Your business now. Emily told me." Then he shuffled to the door and left.

Before the door closed, an elderly woman hobbled inside.

"Welcome to Em's." The parrot flew from the counter to the woman's shoulder.

"So good to see you again, Squirrel." With palsied fingers, she stroked the bird's green head.

Emery frowned. "The parrot's name is Squirrel?"

"Things are not always what they seem." The old woman's hazel eyes shifted to Emery. "I can see the resemblance. Yes, you are Emily's niece. I'm Triana."

Emery admired the elaborate embroidery of the old woman's blouse and long skirt. She found it difficult to pull her eyes away from the swirling patterns of gold and silver threads. Glancing at Triana's wizen face, she nodded. "I'm Emery Lofton."

"Emily told me you would be running the shop. She knew—"

"Hold on. I'm closing the business and selling the building."

The old woman chortled. "You were born to do this. The shop was named for you."

"No, it was named for Aunt Emily."

Laughing even louder, the old woman said, "She spoke of you often. Always called you Em."

"I have a job to go back to," Emery protested, even if she hated being a lawyer.

"This is your job now. Each item must be matched with the right owner. That's the magical part of being here. Every match is a reason to celebrate."

"Like the dragon tooth for that little man?"

"Exactly."

Being a shopkeeper had never occurred to her, but she wasn't happy working for the law firm.

"Come with me." Triana led her to a tapestry on the wall. "Pull this back."

Emery grasped the heavy fabric and lifted it, exposing a hidden door.

"Go in." The old woman pointed with a shaky arm. "It's all yours."

Emery opened the door, and her eyes widened. "It's so colorful!"

Clusters of balloons in a rainbow of hues floated near the ceiling. Jars of brightly colored jellybeans sat next to jars of buttons in assorted sizes and shades. Blooming plants with bright flowers cascaded in fragrant clumps. Everywhere she turned, a surprise caught her attention.

Triana hobbled to Emery's side. "Everything must be placed with the right recipient. The magic won't work otherwise. There is danger if magic gets in the wrong hands."

"That's a big responsibility." She weighed the implications.

"You can do it."

A butterfly landed on Emery's hand. As she considered a new career, her smile grew. Aunt Emily had planned for her to take this over. "I need to cancel the realtor. Em's Shop of Magical Wonders is open for business."

The Story Behind the Story for "Em's Shop of Magical Wonders"

In June of 2025, my local library announced an opportunity for young writers and adults to submit a short story of up to 1,000 words on the theme of "colorful." I knew exactly the short story I wanted to write.

The very first time I read about a new fantasy subgenre called cozy fantasy I was intrigued. A cozy fantasy is a heartwarming tale with low-level stakes, in contrast to an epic fantasy, which typically involves high-stakes battles and major conflicts. I read several novels that were categorized as cozy fantasy. Honestly, I found them rather boring. But still was haunted with the idea that I could write an engaging cozy fantasy.

The story that formed in my head centered around a young woman who inherited her aunt's shop but soon discovered the inventory included magical wonders. This short piece is the potential opening for a longer novel where various customers and magic items may reveal a bigger challenge. If I'm writing this cozy fantasy, it won't be boring!

Since several of my novels started from a short story, time will tell if Em's shop turns into something longer.

The Magic
of
Outer Space

Coming to Terms

Inside her quarters on the orbital space platform, Senior Negotiator Harza Alton queried her neural databank for her vital signs. Normal body temp. Increased heart rate. Elevated pulse. Taking a deep breath, she quieted her thoughts. The hastily scheduled commlink from Conglomerate headquarters had unsettled her more than she expected.

"For five Earth years, I've sent progress reports to management on negotiations with the Elders of Hebron," she muttered to herself. "In all that time, corporate never bothered to get involved. Now, with the agreement in its final evolution, what could be so urgent to require an extended commlink?"

The soft voice of the databank thrummed in her brain instantly. Sixty-four monthly status updates relayed to Planetary Extraction Conglomerate's schedule drive. Reports included major events and significant obstacles.

Management responses limited to brief inquiries, positive reaction, award of 1,435,190 credits posted to Harza Alton's asset account, and promotion to Senior Negotiator level.

"Thanks for reminding me," Harza said. Although she could respond mentally, the quaint practice of responding verbally to the databank made the conversation more natural, a practice she had started when the databank was implanted on her fifth birthday.

Do you want a response to your inquiry?

She frowned. "What?"

The personal databank's even tone continued. High probability the top priority commlink is due to the final terms agreed upon with the Hebron Council. The agreement is in its final form and recorded in main covenant system. Ten Earth minutes to network connection.

"But this sure doesn't feel like a 'Congratulations, job well done' communication, especially after the Division Lead told his superior, I was out of control." Harza strode from the platform's residence quarters and headed toward the network chamber. The noise-deadening flooring silenced the sound of her footsteps.

Behavior of Conglomerate Division Lead Gimpet is unexplainable. Outside forces or incomplete information may be responsible. Probability of negative commlink encounter is 98.75 percent. Eight minutes to network connection.

Harza's chest tightened. She was in trouble but could not explain why. The agreement was a decent outcome to a long and often difficult negotiation. Sure, there were some concessions. How else could she convince the Hebrons to allow the massive disturbance of their planet? All so Conglomerate could mine the valuable ramarin ore? But she had been careful to advise headquarters on the most critical elements of the agreement. She had worked so long to reach this point.

"It's a fine agreement," Harza whispered to herself, mentally warning the databank not to comment.

She stopped in front of the sealed security lock and scanned her identification card. After straightening her shoulders, she lifted her chin and entered the day's clearance code. The door slid open with a soft whirr and a rush of disinfected air. As she passed through the entry sensors, she blinked at the familiar tingle of the chromosomal scan.

Quickly, she selected a seat before a small monitor, bypassing the large wall screen. Once logged into the system, she settled into the ergonomic seat and adjusted the lighting to soften her graying hair and wrinkles.

"Welcome, Senior Negotiator Alton." The monitor's greeting screen morphed to the blue Conglomerate logo. "Your comlink will begin in two minutes. Please stand by."

She struggled to ease the tension in her jaw and still her thoughts. "Relax. Herronib, herronbo," she chanted. The Hebron manta she had learned five years ago flowed through her being, and she inhaled deeply.

The monitor flashed a countdown clock across the screen. When it reached zero, the weathered face of Command Torric Spar replaced the Conglomerate logo.

"Alton." Spar's crisp voice bellowed through the chamber. "You're a disgrace to the Negotiation Corps. This agreement is full of unacceptable terms and counter to our business interests." As he spoke, his face reddened and the vein along his temple protruded. "You were never qualified to assume responsibility for this negotiation. I knew it and objected to your placement in such a critical role. And clearly, I was right."

Harza blinked rapidly and tightened her hands into fists. Stay in control, she told herself. Her heart raced and she stiffened in the console seat.

"Command Spar—"

"Your judgement is of no value to the Conglomerate. Anyone who would agree to thermal and particulate atmospheric sampling without regard to the cost of such nonsense is useless."

"But the Hebron Council insisted," Harza protested. "Division Lead Gimpet was there when the Council threatened to cease negotiations. He knows I tried for three Earth months to eliminate that requirement. And there still may be a way to reduce the cost of monitoring."

"Enough, Alton." The blood vessels along Spar's temples throbbed faster. "This agreement is a disgrace for us, and you're to blame. The agreement is now part of the universal document catalog, so it's impossible for us to change the outcome. But I can change your responsibilities. Your reassignment has been sent to your databank." The screen went blank.

Harza sat in shock, staring at the slowly rotating disconnected symbol. How could this happen? She closed her eyes, fighting to control her emotions.

"I did my best," she said in an angry voice.

The databank thrummed rapidly. ACKNOWLEDGED RECEIPT OF COMMAND SPAR MESSAGE. DO YOU WISH TO LISTEN TO IT NOW? The vibration paused.

"No," Harza snapped, launching herself upright from the console seat. She ground her teeth together and stormed to the sealed door. Her finger hesitated above the access panel. She willed herself to inhale slowly. Then, she eased the muscles across her back. "What's the message?"

REASSIGNED IMMEDIATELY TO STAR SYSTEM DEVON MINOR. RESOLVE PROTOCOL DISPUTE OVER RENEWAL OF MINING RIGHTS. DEPARTURE IS SCHEDULED TODAY ABOARD SPACE CRUISER BETA. DETAILED ITINERARY FOLLOWS. The databank signaled completion of the message. SHALL I REPORT SPECIFICS?

"No. Is there anything more?"

PRESENT PERFORMANCE RATING IS MARGINAL, RISK LEVEL RED. DEMOTED TO JUNIOR NEGOTIATOR. The databank ended with an empathetic hum.

Harza lifted her chin and fingered the exit code. She stepped past the security sensor and headed toward the nearest walkway. She wandered the passages of the platform, lost in an evaluation of options. Finally, she returned to her quarters and packed a few personal items.

FIFTY-FIVE EARTH MINUTES TO LOADING FOR INTERSHIP TRANSPORT.

"I'm going to the Relax Deck. Remind me of the departure time fifteen minutes before loading."

NOTIFICATION SCHEDULED. TAKE YOUR TIME AT THE RELAX DECK. The databank purred.

Harza smiled at the human attributes of the neural device. Programming on these units must be nearing self-realization level. Its voice often seemed to sense her emotions.

In a few minutes, Harza arrived at the welcome chamber of the Relax Deck. She scanned the menu of activities and selected the refreshment room. The door to her right slid open with a whine, and she entered cautiously, peering around to see who she might encounter.

Two men shared a table near the star chart at the far end of the room. One of them waved to her.

"Harza! Come celebrate with us," the large man yelled across the room.

"What are you celebrating, Berk?" Harza slipped into the empty seat between her two coworkers.

"Our successful negotiation, of course." Mineralogist Berk Lamberg searched Harza's face. "To a completed agreement." He raised his glass and downed the brown liquid.

As a robotic attendant approached their table, bespeckled Engineer Tech Rim Pento asked, "What would you like to drink, Harza? One of those fuzzy Hebron drinks?"

She half-smiled. "I'm ready for something stronger today. Maybe a Cretian Flash."

The attendant nodded and left.

Both Berk and Rim stared at her.

"I'll have plenty of time for the effects to wear off," she said. "I've been reassigned to Devon Minor."

"No," Berk roared.

Rim reached over and grasped Harza's arm. "Why?"

"Spar's unhappy with the agreement. Called it a disgrace."

"Doesn't he realize how much work and effort went into that agreement?" Berk sputtered. "It's a blazing victory for Conglomerate."

The attendant returned with the round of drinks and set a tall thin glass of bright red alcohol blend before Harza.

"To friends." Harza raised her glass and looked at Berk and Rim. The first sip filled her eyes with tears, which she quickly wiped away.

"Blasted Spar." Berk stared at the foam at the top of his drink. "Devon Minor's a backwater. You belong here. This is going to be a complex extraction, and no one knows the agreement terms like you do. Plus, the Hebron leaders trust you."

Rim drank his Tripol brandy quickly. "Sounds like Gimpet let things get out of hand with Spar."

The Cretian Flash loosened Harza's muscles. "I kept Gimpet informed about everything. It wasn't my responsibility to report to Spar. That's what Gimpet was supposed to do. I just don't know what happened." She took another sip of the almost empty beverage.

"He's a useless piece of space debris," Berk thundered.

"You don't have to take Spar's treatment, Harza." Rim reached over, cupping her chin in his hand. "You're too good to be treated like this."

"I already put a Free Space message on the Career Board. There just aren't any openings right now for experienced negotiators. And I need the credits from Conglomerate to keep Moki and Cosay enrolled in the Academy."

The three silently studied their empty glasses.

"My biggest regret," Harza said with a sigh, "was that I missed so much of their growing up. Now, they're both in Academy, and I devoted the last five years to Hebron."

The robotic attendant returned to refresh drinks. Berk and Rim nodded for another round.

"Fifteen Earth minutes to loading at Gate 3." The databank repeated the message two more times while Harza ignored the warning.

She squeezed Berk's burly hand. "I really enjoyed working with you. Be careful during the extraction."

Berk nodded.

"And you." She turned to Rim. "Thank you for everything. You taught me a lot."

"You were an easy student, Harza." He paused. "You did something incredible here."

"I know," she sighed and rose to leave. After hugging each man, she hurried to the loading area at the platform's transport level.

The transit to Star Cruiser Beta and the insertion into the sleep chamber on the ship were a blur to Harza. She battled her demons during the power down stage, under the watchful monitoring of a medix-computer which injected additional relaxants into her chamber.

Harza roused three solar cycles later as the Star Cruiser Beta eased into the open berth at Station Eclipse, in orbit around Devon Minor. After clearance from the medix-computer, the sleep chamber opened, and

Harza left its cocoon-like comfort. She joined the crowd of travelers shuffling to the disembark area.

The sting of her dismissal from Hebron nagged in the far recesses of her mind, but the prolonged period of sleep travel had numbed her pain. Harza puzzled over her new assignment. While she waited in line for travel processing, she quizzed her databank about what she had missed.

GREETINGS, HARZA ALTON. The databank had acquired a tenor voice and sounded almost human. SIX MESSAGES AWAIT YOUR REVIEW. ONE FROM COMMAND TORRIC SPAR. TWO EACH FROM MOKI AND COSAY. ONE FROM MEDOR, CONGLOMERATE AMBASSADOR TO DEVON MINOR COMPLEX. ORIENTATION INFORMATION ON DEVON MINOR COMPLEX HAS BEEN LOADED INTO MY MEMORY. UPGRADE OF MY COMMUNICATION CIRCUITS WAS COMPLETED IN TRANSIT. DO YOU WISH TO LISTEN TO YOUR MESSAGES NOW?

"No. Let's get through this blasted processing first. They can whisk us across the universe in less time than it takes to unload passengers from this crate." She frowned at the bitterness in her voice. She had acquired a new tone, too.

Harza spent most of the day completing security checks and health screenings, before settling into the Eclipse's accommodations for those in transit. The plain interior of the cubicle suited her current mood. Reclining in the meditation center of the room, she reviewed her messages.

COMMAND SPAR SAYS HE'S PLEASED WITH THE WAY YOU HAVE TAKEN THE REASSIGNMENT. The databank hummed slightly.

"What else could I do?" Harza clenched her jaw. "Continue with replay."

Your son, Moki, reported his advancement through Academy. That message was sent just as you entered the Beta's sleep chamber. The second message from Moki arrived shortly before docking with Station Eclipse. He reports the successful completion of Academy in three Earth years and a position with the Space Transport Authority.

Harza smiled at the thought of her freckled-face son piloting a Star Cruiser one day. "Send him my congratulations and request a commlink with him at his convenience." She mused about the boy she had not seen grow up.

Shall I continue? the databank asked.

"Yes. What are Cosay's messages?"

Both messages express her concern for you and ask about your activities.

"Cosay would be a good Negotiator. She cares." Harza closed her eyes and rubbed her temples. You can care too much. After a moment, she asked, "And what is she doing now?"

Cosay was enrolled in Academy but elected to join a colonization forced headed to the Asimov Sector. She owes a large debt to the Global Council for her Pioneer License.

Harza sighed at the endless cycle of indebtedness. Wasn't it the cost of guaranteeing an Academy education for both her children that had led her to work for Conglomerate and taken her away from them long ago? If Cosay had selected the noble cause of pioneering in some unknow portion of the universe, that was her right. Harza hoped the outcome would be more satisfying than her Hebron experience.

"Compare the cost of Academy to Pioneer License."

As the databank calculated, Harza rose from the recliner and stretched until her joints cracked. How old was she now?

Calculation complete. The full cost of training at the Academy—

"No! Just the difference." The angry edge to her voice startled her.

Pioneer License is 62,500 credits more than Academy.

"That's not as bad as I thought it would be. The Devon assignment should cover that with a little to spare." Harza removed her travel suit, letting it drop to the floor, and headed to the cleansing receptacle.

Incoming message from Medor.

She frowned. "Who's that?"

Conglomerate Ambassador to Devon Minor Complex.

"Oh, yes. Briefly, what was his previous message?"

Words of welcome and pleasure at your upcoming arrival. The current message is coded urgent. The databank throbbed with a sharp insistence.

"Accept the incoming message and request a private connection. No video." This would be a first, she thought, standing naked.

"Greetings, Ambassador Medor. Junior Negotiator Harza Alton prepared to assist you." She grimaced as she declared her lower rank title.

The databank converted her words into galactic superspace frequencies.

After a prolonged silence, the databank whirred. "Ambassador Medor seems agitated. He reports your help is needed immediately.

Notify him when you are on planet. I relayed your remaining travel specifics. He awaits you at Conglomerate's main facility on Devon Minor."

"Summarize the nature of my assignment. I can't imagine what all the hurry is about. No wait. I'll get to this matter when I've finished bathing." She returned to the cleansing unit and programmed a long, penetrating vibra-steam. She relaxed in the swirling mist and vowed not to become so involved in whatever problem was on Devon Minor. No need to repeat the painful lesson from Hebron. This time would be different.

When the planetary shuttle emerged from the green clouds that shrouded Devon Minor and landed at the central terminal, Harza was surprised to find Ambassador Medor waiting to greet her personally. The portly gentleman shook her hand vigorously, and seemed relieved—almost overjoyed—to see her.

"I have heard such wonderful things about you, Negotiator Alton. I understand you're the one who gained approval for the Conglomerate to core Hebron. What a great accomplishment."

You obviously haven't spoken to Spar, she thought. She merely replied, "Thank you."

The next days, weeks, and months were devoted to learning the customs and culture of Devon Minor. She enjoyed exploring the finer points of the society's essence. Such understanding added to her ability to negotiate and reach settlements.

Ambassador Medor applauded Harza for her willingness to master the clicks and guttural sounds of the native language. For her part, she did it numbly, more out of habit earned from years of negotiating. Somehow, nothing on Devon Minor measured up to the challenges of Hebron.

"Nicely done, Harza." Ambassador Medor's grin widened as she reported on the successful completion of the Devon renewal.

"The Conglomerate will be allowed to extract Devon ores for another three Earth centuries. In exchange for that exclusive right, we must provide Devonians with a culture expansion center and train the indigenous population in the universal communication system. The Devon Minor Committee of Elect were quite adamant the inhabitants be left with useful skills after the ore supply is exhausted." Harza steeled herself for an adverse reaction.

Ambassador Medor pulled at his lower lip. "Seems like a reasonable request. The value of the ore will far exceed any costs to train and educate the locals." He paused and grasped Harza's hand. "And exclusive rights for three hundred years is much more than we expected. You've done an excellent job." In his enthusiasm, the Ambassador forgot protocol and kissed Harza on the cheek. "I must report the outcome to management. Great pulsars, Harza. This is superlative!"

"The agreement can be recorded as soon as Conglomerate accepts the Devon terms," Harza said in a steady tone. She appreciated the Ambassador's excitement but the negotiation had been very easy. The

Devonians were light years behind the Hebrons in terms of sophistication and greed.

Ambassador Medor, a broad smile beaming from his round face, hurried to his office. She doubted Command Spar would approve any of the agreement terms that cost Conglomerate any of its profit. Rather than following the Ambassador, she returned to her quarters.

Harza sat back and viewed the video transmittal her daughter had sent recently from the pioneer colony now established in the Asimov Sector. Cosay's narrative conveyed her passion for the settlement effort on the dry and dusty planet.

She remembered her own enthusiasm when she first visited Hebron. "I guess I'll never see Hebron again." Lost in her reflections, she missed the initial incoming message pulsed by her databank.

SCRAMBLED INCOMING MESSAGE FROM COSAY. CODED CONFIDENTIAL AND URGENT. IMMEDIATE REPLY REQUESTED.

"Accept the message and translate." Harza paced the confines of her quarters and imagined a variety of accidents that might have befallen her daughter far across the distant reaches of space.

Her databank descrambled the coded message and replayed with a warm tone. Cosay is well and extremely excited.

Once again, Harza wondered whether the databank could sense emotions.

SHE REPORTS THE DISCOVERY OF AN UNKNOWN MINERAL ON THE PLANET. THE PIONEERS HAVE COLONY RIGHTS TO THE ORE. SHE ASKS THAT YOU JOIN THEM. HER EXACT WORDS ARE 'MOTHER, WE NEED A NEGOTIATOR OF YOUR SKILL TO PROTECT US IN DEALING WITH CONGLOMERATE.' SHE REQUESTS YOUR TIMELY RESPONSE.

Harza relaxed, relieved her worries about a catastrophic accident were unfounded. Then she frowned. "Leave Comglomerate to negotiate on behalf of a pioneer planet? Represent the other side in a negotiation?" She puzzled over the implications. "But I've worked for Conglomerate most of my life."

The databank pulsed with another incoming message. MINERALOGIST BECK LAMBERG ADVISES YOUR REPLACEMENT ON HEBRON HAS OFFENDED THE ELDERS. THEY ARE DEMANDING YOUR RETURN. COMMAND SPAR IS NO LONGER RESPONSIBLE FOR HEBRON. YOU CAN GO BACK BUT REMAIN A JUNIOR NEGOTIATOR.

Closing her eyes, Harza considered her situation. Returning to Hebron where she had spent so much time, would allow her to be part of the coring team to implement the terms of the agreement. She struggled with her pain and anger in the way she had been dismissed.

A request for entrance at the door to her quarters interrupted her thoughts. "Harza. It's me, Ambassador Medor. May I enter?"

She welcomed him to her Devon apartment but noticed his agitation.

"Conglomerate headquarters wasn't as pleased with the outcome of the negotiations as I thought they would be," he said. "Training indigenous population would set a precedent they're afraid might become expected elsewhere. They want the agreement revised."

Harza shook her head and smiled ruefully. "Is it too much for the people of Devon Minor to ask that after the mineral resources of their planet are extracted, they be left with some basic skills so they can continue to deal with trade in the universal marketplace?"

He shrugged his portly shoulders. "They want you to renegotiate the agreement."

"Well." Harza's smile broadened, and she stood confidently. "They'll have to find someone else to do it. I have another negotiation to begin—and Conglomerate won't find it an easy agreement to reach—especially when I represent the other side."

She shook the Ambassador's hand and escorted the startled man to the door. Then removed the Conglomerate pin on her shirt.

"Get me the earliest transport to the Asimov Sector," she said to her databank.

The unit responded immediately. ALREADY BOOKED YOU ABOARD THE STAR CRUISER EXPLORER III, COPILOTED BY MOKI ALTON. ALSO SIGNALED COSAY ALTON THAT YOU ARE ON YOUR WAY.

A joyful vibration filled her head.

Harza laughed, convinced the databank had assumed human emotions. "Let's go negotiate." She felt free, suddenly years younger. "And see my children."

The Story Behind the Story for "Coming to Terms"

"Coming to Terms" is an unpublished story written in 1994 or 1995. It was submitted to *The Magazine of Fantasy & Science Fiction* and *Asimov's Science Fiction* magazine shortly after it was written but not accepted by either publication. After that, it was put away and forgotten.

In a way, it is my most autobiographical story. In the early 1990s, my job involved negotiating regulatory approvals for a large project. All approvals were unanimous. What should have been a personal success and career builder was questioned by upper management at the end of the approval process. "Coming to Terms" was written to release the frustration and anxiety I felt at the time.

When I decided to include "Coming to Terms" in this collection, I had to rewrite parts of it because the futuristic technology I had envisioned in mid-1990s has since become today's standard technology. A neural databank replaced the personal databank clipped to a belt. At the time I wrote the original, I never imagined the many functions current phones now perform.

The Magic
of
Spirits

Spirits of the Land

INSIDE THE ELEVATED CAB of the dragline excavator, Mitch examined the sandy scrubland below. He positioned the boom for the initial excavation at Chemco's New Hope Mine.

Slowly, he lowered the giant bucket and dragged it along the ground. The metal teeth ripped through the grass, scooping up topsoil. As Mitch raised the load, clods of dirt fell to the ground. A dark shape beyond the bucket, followed by several more, caught his attention. He stopped the dragline suddenly and radioed, "Boss, there's still cows out here."

A stern voice crackled through the cab's speaker. "Nonsense. Get digging!"

"I just saw a cowboy cracking a whip behind a herd of cattle." Mitch peered out the window, but the rider and cows were gone.

The next cut was deeper into the excavation. The sodden soil clung to the broad mouth of the bucket. Mitch rubbed his eyes before he stopped the dragline again. He counted the figures passing the bucket. With a shaking hand, he toggled the radio. "Boss, honest to God, it's Indians. They walked right in front of me. Three of them."

"Have you been drinking, Mitch? Get going or you're fired!"

After a ragged sigh, Mitch guided the bucket back into the hole for the next cut. It tore deeper into the earth, exposing phosphate ore. A massive creature with long tusks rose from the ground.

"A woolly mammoth," Mitch whispered, watching the shaggy beast advance toward the dragline. He felt the machine shake with each footstep, and then the ground opened below the mining rig. The excavator tumbled with a metallic groan. Mitch's scream was lost in the darkness.

The accident report read: "Sinkhole developed under dragline. One fatality." It never mentioned cattle, Indians or prehistoric creatures. But when the miners get together at Tooskie's Bar, they talk in low tones about Mitch and the spirits of the land.

The Story Behind the Story for "Spirits of the Land"

Flash fiction was a new concept when "Spirits of the Land" was written in 1995. At that time, a Florida State University writing contest set a 250-word limit for a one-page short short story. This piece was submitted for the contest but did not win. For inclusion in this collection, I've added a few more sensory details to enrich the setting.

In the early 1990s, I had been working on a large project that involved land previously mined by the phosphate industry. The large dragline machines with their massive buckets for digging made quite an impression. I imagined what would happen if history came to life as the dragline excavated deeper into the earth.

The Spanish
Moss Picker

RECKON I WAS ABOUT ten when Pa sent me to stay with Grandpap for the summer—the summer of 1930.

"A young one ought to know how to fish, milk a cow, and gut a chicken," Pa told me. Just like he had done as a kid. Pa says if things don't improve soon, I'll be working in the factory with him, so I best enjoy this time.

Grandpap and Grandmam lived near the shore of Lake Tsala Apopka, in a cabin nestled under the canopy of a live oak hammock. The nearest place where I could get a bottle of soda pop was a town called Floral City.

I remember one particular evening of that summer real well. At the end of a hot, muggy day, Grandpap and I sat on the front porch after dinner. Perched on a large rocking chair, I swung my bare feet and swattered at the blood-thirsty mosquitos. Grandpap sipped his sweet tea and puffed on a cigar. The smell was strong enough to keep the skeeters away from him. We watched a heron hunting for tadpoles in the water until the sun set and the sky darkened.

Grandpap loved telling stories. I sometimes thought Pa wanted me to hear Grandpap's tales more than learn to live in the wilds of Florida's swamp. Seemed like Grandpap spent more time storytelling than fishing when we went out on the lake. The catfish I caught today had started him on a tale about the monster fish that got away.

Tonight, he was in the middle of recounting how an old Florida cowboy lassoed an alligator, when the night air was cut by a loud screech. I sat straight up and stopped rocking.

"What's that?" My eyes widened and scanned the growing darkness around the cabin.

"Could be a coyote." Grandpap blew out a cloud of smoke. The lit end of his cigar glowed orange in the night air. "Some people claim when you hear a shriek in the night, it's the spirit of the Spanish Moss Picker."

I leaned closer to Grandpap. "A ghost?"

"Don't rightly know, but the story of the Spanish Moss Picker been around a long, long time. Ain't your pa told you about him?"

I shook my head and brushed a buzzing mosquito away from my ear.

Grandpap raised his glass and drained the last of its contents. "Irene, gonna need more tea. This youngster wants to know the story about the picker."

From inside, Grandmam called back. "Don't be giving that boy nightmares."

A moment later, she opened the screen door and refilled Grandpap's glass. With a smile, she handed me a slice of watermelon and wiped her hand on her apron. She smelled like fresh baked bread and the fried catfish we had for dinner.

"Don't you worry yourself about this old man's stories of spirits and such nonsense," she said and tousled my hair before going back inside. The screen door banged shut behind her.

The watermelon was sweet, and I spit a seed into the leaves beyond the porch. A lizard scurried away at the disturbance.

I waited for Grandpap to tell me about the spirit. I'd seen plenty of the silvery-gray clumps of Spanish moss hanging from the live oak trees and swaying in the wind. It looked so peaceful dangling from the branches. What kind of ghost could haunt it?

Grandpap tapped the ash off the end of his cigar and coughed. "Now where were we?"

"The Spanish Moss Picker." I must have sounded eager, because Grandpap laughed.

"Don't know if this is true, but folks swear it is."

I settled back in the rocking chair and took another bite of the watermelon. Grandpap's stories always started the same way. As if warning the listener got him off the hook. Believe at your own risk.

"It was long ago, when a young feller named Walter left the big city up north to make his fortune in Florida. He rode the train as far south as his money allowed. That being Floral City. It was a busy place back then. Lots of workers mining phosphate."

Another howl cut through the air, and I nearly jumped from my seat. I listened closely but only heard an alligator bellow, a chorus of frogs, and a raccoon digging in the leaves.

"Well, Walter wanted to make enough money to attract and marry a certain young lady he met when he got off the train. With his city ways, mining didn't fit his idea of making a fortune. When he met Earl, he was ready to listen to a get-rich-quick way."

Grandpap took a gulp of sweet tea, followed by a puff on his cigar.

"What was the way?" I asked.

"Earl told him that he would make lots of money picking Spanish moss. It was gold waiting to be harvested."

"How can that be? It grows all over the place."

Grandpap chuckled. "Seems Walter wasn't smart enough to realize that. See, back then, they used it for packing items to ship and to stuff mattresses, pillows, and seats."

"I didn't know that."

"Walter got a couple of burlap sacks and set out to fill them full of Spanish moss. He probably thought it was easy money. He picked up all the moss he saw lying on the ground and filled his bags. To make room for more, he rolled up his shirt sleeves and pushed the moss down into the bottom of each burlap bag. Soon, he couldn't fit any more in the sacks and headed back to find Earl. On the way back, his arms started itching something fierce. He scratched and scratched until his arms were a bloody mess."

The mosquito buzzed by my ear again and landed on the back of my neck. I slapped at it, but not before it bit me. I rubbed the spot and started itching. I felt for Walter.

After a pull on his cigar, Grandpap continued, "Some call them red bugs, others chiggers."

In the light slipping through the cabin window, I saw Grandpap shake his head.

"Nasty biters, those chiggers," he said.

The thought of them burrowing into my arms made me itch harder. "What happened next?"

"He carried those sacks to Earl, but when Earl saw Walter's arms, he didn't want to pay him. Earl scolded him for picking Spanish moss from the ground rather than from the trees. That being why it was full of bugs."

I stopped scratching my neck. "There're no chiggers in the stuff hanging from the branches?"

"Nope." Grandpap yawned. "Walter went to visit Ruthie to let her know he was still working to make a fortune so they could get married. She wouldn't let him in the house 'cause his arms looked so awful."

"That wasn't very nice." Girls were not of much interest to me, but her not letting him inside seemed kind of mean. I spit out a couple more watermelon seeds.

"Walter borrowed a cart from her father and went off to collect more moss. This time, he pulled it off the lower branches. He had to go pretty far out of town 'cause all the easy-to-collect moss was gone. It was hot, so he took off his shirt and climbed the trees."

Grandpap chuckled. "This northern dandy didn't respect the Florida sun. Pretty soon, he was redder than a cardinal. Must have hurt something terrible. He was gone for several days. When he returned, the cart was overflowing with bundles of Spanish moss. He went straight to Ruthie's house to show her how hard he had worked to make money for their wedding. Dang! She screamed when she saw how red his face was. He went off broken-hearted and determined to make enough to buy her a ring."

"Did he go back to Earl?"

"He sure did. But this time the snake oil salesman eyed the cart and paid him a penny for all the work."

I frowned. "What's a snake oil salesman?"

"Anyone you can't trust. That there Earl was slippery like a snake. Walter was disappointed with the pay for all the days he spent picking moss from the trees. He complained, and Earl told him the pay would've been more if he had brought back blue Spanish moss."

"Grandpap, I've never seen blue Spanish moss."

"Me neither. But Earl told him it grew at the very top of the tree, close to the sky. That city feller believed him and went back out into the woods with the cart. He climbed to the top of the highest oak tree. His clothes got caught on branches and ripped. But guess what?"

I squirmed in my seat, trying to figure out what he found up there. "I don't know. What?"

Grandpap laughed. "Nothing, nothing at all. Weren't much Spanish moss that high up. And what was there wasn't blue. Walter finally figured out that Earl was making a fool out of him, and he was mad. He hurried down the tree but fell. He bumped from branch to branch, getting cut and scraped and banged up."

"Ouch. That had to hurt," I said.

With a snort, Grandpap slapped his leg. "You bet. That poor guy was a mess. He limped back to town and went straight to Ruthie's house. Earl was there. Seems that while Walter was gone, Earl and Ruthie got married."

I had little use for girls, but that didn't sit well with me.

"Walter grabbed Earl by the collar and dragged him into the woods. It was getting mighty dark by then. Witnesses said they saw Ruthie run after them. All three of them disappeared into the swamp. Sometime later that night, they heard a God-awful scream. They couldn't tell who made the terrifying noise. None of the three of them was ever seen again. Over the years, the common belief is it's the spirit of the Spanish Moss Picker we hear. Although I reckon it could be any one of them."

The howl sounded again, and I listened to the plaintive cry, wondering which one of the three it sounded like.

"Or, it could be a coyote," Grandpap said. He tossed the stub of his cigar to the porch floor and ground it under his boot heel.

"Time for bed," Grandmam called through the screen door. "If you can sleep after that story."

"Just remember," Grandpap pointed a finger at me. "Don't be fooled by snake oil salesman or you too could become a lesson for some future youngster."

Reckon Pa sent me to learn a lesson like that, in addition to fishing and spitting out watermelon seeds.

Originally published in *Spirits of Florida's Nature Coast*, Citrus Writers of Florida, 2024.

The Story Behind the Story for "The Spanish Moss Picker"

This story was first published in an anthology called *Spirits of Florida's Nature Coast*, produced by the Citrus Writers of Florida non-profit.

The idea for the story emerged after a visit to the Floral City Heritage Museum. One of the exhibits was a mill for processing Spanish moss to use for packing material and stuffing mattresses and other items. The museum also provided information about the history of Floral City and how the area developed. Some of that information is included in the story. For instance, phosphate mining was a major activity in Floral City prior to World War I, and the community had railroad service during the timeframe established in the story.

I spend time picking Spanish moss from the live oak trees on my property, not for processing, but to keep it away from the places where I ride my horses. With so much firsthand experience, it was natural to use this plant that hangs from tree branches for a story.

The Brooksville Watch Cat

Ask any old timer in Brooksville, and they'll tell you to be on the lookout for the watch cat, a sturdy black feline with four white paws, a white face, and a scarred ear. Something important is about to happen when you see him. After that, he'll disappear for a long time.

The first report of the cat occurred in 1890, when he showed up at the Brooksville train depot. Station Master Tom Randall noted the event in his log, but if you talked to him after hours, he added more details.

The January morning started like any other day, with Tom preparing for the 10:15 from Ocala. He checked the time on his pocket watch against the Seth Thomas regulator clock mounted on the wall. He frowned and scratched his forehead. Thirty minutes difference between the two timepieces. They never agreed, and he wasn't sure which was right.

The railroad management had warned him he would lose his job if there were any more delays in Brooksville departures. Tom was determined to avoid getting fired because of minutes lost in boarding passengers and loading freight. The train must leave on time.

He readied the mail pouch and inventoried the crates to be sent south. The nip in the waiting room air reminded him to toss more coal in the stove. He glanced at the regulator again. The pendulum swung steadily to the rhythmic ticktock of the clock. The minute hand pointed at six.

A gentleman in a brown derby and a woman in a green dress hurried through the door. A gust of cold air and a large cat followed them inside. The cat marched toward the warm stove, circled once, and curled into a ball.

"Have we missed the train?" The man tapped his fingers against the ticket counter.

"No, sir. It should arrive soon."

All eyes turned to the clock on the wall.

"It's late." The man removed his derby and brushed dust off its brim.

Tom checked his pocket watch again. "Not according to this." He extended his watch in the man's direction to show the watch hands at ten o'clock.

The cat lifted his broad head and meowed, a deep guttural sound. A minute later, a train whistle sounded in the distance.

"Please have your tickets ready for boarding," Tom announced. "The train from Ocala will arrive shortly."

As the locomotive rumbled into the station, Tom focused on completing his loading and boarding activities. He opened the door to the platform for the departing passengers and greeted the arrivals. The temperatures had risen slightly, but the winter air still sent a chill through his body.

After the train left, Tom returned to the waiting room to warm himself by the stove and chase the cat outside. To his surprise, the cat was gone. He searched the office and the freight area, but there was no sign of the tuxedo kitty. Tom shrugged and thought nothing more about it until the next day, when the cat made another appearance just before the train arrived.

Some days, there were no passengers, and the station was quiet, except for the ticking of the clock. On those days, Tom spoke to the cat. "If you're going to be a regular here, you need a name." He peered at the manufacturer's name on the face of the clock. "How about Seth? You're my best timekeeper."

Every morning, Tom set out a bowl of water and leftovers from his dinner, watching for the cat. Seth arrived with his confident stride, ate the food, and rubbed his black body against Tom's legs. The Station Master scratched the broad, mostly white head. "You're a solid old man, Seth."

Day after day, Tom came to count on the cat's accuracy in announcing the incoming train and his disappearance when the train was gone. Tom's boss even complimented him on how the departures from Brooksville were running smoothly.

Then one morning, Seth paced around the waiting room and wouldn't settle on the blanket Tom had placed on the floor near the stove. The cat meowed repeatedly. Tom glanced at the wall clock and double-checked his watch.

"It's too early for the Ocala train," Tom said, more to himself than to the cat.

Seth yowled and ran to the door leading to the platform. He clawed at the wood frame. The cat's behavior worried Tom.

A screech and a loud rumble boomed in the distance. The glass in the depot windows rattled. One passenger in the waiting room opened the door to investigate, and Seth raced outside.

A few minutes later, a rider on a horse galloped to the depot and rushed inside. The boy's face was pale, his eyes open wide. Tom hurried to his side.

"The train..." The boy gasped for air. "The train came off the tracks near the river."

Tom hurried to the platform. He spotted a rising curl of smoke to the north, but the cat was nowhere to be seen.

When stories of the train derailment were told for years afterward, Tom often shared the account of Seth's reaction before the event happened. He always ended with the sad comment, "And I never saw that cat again, even though I watched for him every day"

On May 8, 1945, the Brooksville Mayor hurried to the steps of the Courthouse, waving a telegram. A stream of people followed him. He slowed as he climbed the front steps. At the top step, a black-and-white cat with his tail wrapped around his front legs sat like a statue. The mayor moved his foot to push the cat out of the way. The feline settled into a crouch and closed his eyes.

With a huff, the mayor moved to a lower step. He cleared his throat and in a loud voice said, "It's official. The war in Europe is over."

The crowd cheered and applauded. People danced in the street, and church bells rang. The cat rolled over and stretched, extending the claws of his white paws.

A woman in the crowd pointed at the feline. "Whoever owns that cat should call him Victory."

A reporter snapped a photograph of the mayor with the cat beside him. The image appeared in the newspaper the next day with the caption, "Victory the cat watches the VE announcement."

Despite being a local celebrity, the cat was not seen again until August 14 of that same year, when the mayor climbed the courthouse steps to announce the end of the war in the Pacific. The cat tucked his white paws under his body and meowed while another newspaper photograph was taken. As the gathered crowd thinned, the cat wandered away. Several decades passed before he was seen again.

While 1970s rock and roll music played on the radio, fire fighter Steve Bridger polished the fender of the ladder truck. He sang along to the refrain of a popular Rolling Stones song.

"Glad you're better at putting out fires than singing." Chief Rob Halsey gave a chuckle and slapped Steve on the back. "This truck is going to look great in the parade tomorrow."

"You bet, chief." Steve glanced away from the truck. "Hey, we have a new station mascot." He pointed at the black-and-white cat that strolled through the open door.

The cat purred and rubbed against Steve's leg. Then dropped to the floor and sprawled in a relaxed pose.

"Getting comfortable, old man?" the chief asked.

"Bet he'd like to ride on the truck in the parade," Steve suggested.

"He's black and white, but he isn't a dalmatian." The chief shook his head. "But he looks like a cat I heard stories about when I was a kid. I think he was called a watch cat."

"What's a watch cat?"

The chief rubbed the back of the cat's neck. "People say to watch out when the cat shows up, because a major event is about to happen. Sometimes it's good, sometimes not."

The cat rose and hissed, arching his back. With his black fur puffed up, the cat looked angry.

"Easy there, old man," Steve said.

Suddenly, the fire alarm sounded, and the station burst into a frenzy of activity. Steve and the chief donned their gear, while other firefighters scrambled into the fire engines. With sirens wailing, the trucks raced into the street. As they drove away, Steve spotted the cat scurrying down the sidewalk.

Hours later, when the firefighters returned from the massive fire at the feed processing plant, the cat was gone. Never to be seen until forty years later.

It was Sunday morning in Brooksville. Reverend Jacob bent down and rubbed the white head of the tuxedo cat on the steps of the church. He stroked the scarred ear of the feline. In return, the cat bumped his head against the minister's hand for more attention.

"Since you're here," Reverend Jacob said, "it must be time for me to invite the congregation into today's service." He counted on the cat to remind him when it was time to ring the bells.

Reverend Jacob went into the church with the cat right behind him. After he rang the bells, he prepared to greet his parishioners. The cat curled up on a pew at the back of the church. As people entered, they avoided the sleeping feline. Whispers of "watch cat" filled the nave.

"Friends," Reverend Jacob said from the altar. "This is the most important thing we can do today. We are gathered here to worship our Lord."

In the church's silence, he distinctly heard the purring of the cat, which brought a smile to his face. The cat knew how important this was.

As you travel through the streets of Brooksville, if you see a black-and-white cat scurrying down the street or around the corner, perhaps it's the Brooksville watch cat. Something important is about to happen.

Originally published in *Booksville: Poetry Anthology and Folktales*, 2025.

The Story Behind the Story for "The Brooksville Watch Cat"

In January 2025, the Brooksville Women's Club held an inaugural author event called Booksville. As part of the program, they invited local authors to submit a false folktale featuring Brooksville for publication in a Booksville anthology.

To generate an idea for a folktale, I visited the library to research Brooksville history and found a book that included details about the railroad depot (now a museum). The depot had a Seth Thomas railway regulator, which was a very accurate clock. The concept of a cat that was as accurate as a Seth Thomas clock grew from this research.

My barn cats are named Blanche, Rose, and Dorothy, after the characters on the television show *Golden Girls*. A stray male cat showed up several years ago when it was time to feed the horses and cats. He was a sturdy, black and white tuxedo. We named him Stan, since Dorothy is also a black and white tuxedo, and on the television show, Dorothy's ex-husband is Stanley. He served as the model for the "watch cat."

The Magic
of
Relationships

Farrier's Footprints

ROB NICHOLS SQUINTED THROUGH the pickup's windshield at the April sun rising in the sky over Odessa. "Gonna be a hot one today," he said and glanced at his sullen, nine-year-old stepson in the passenger seat. Logan hadn't said a word since leaving the house before daybreak.

He backed the farrier trailer to the barn entrance. "First stop." Rob shut off the engine and checked the list of horses he would be doing at the barn. "We have two horses to trim and one that needs shoeing. Remember what I said about being careful around the horses?" When the boy did not reply, Rob took a deep breath. "Your mom told me you have a school questionnaire to fill out."

"I still don't know why I couldn't go with Mom," Logan said.

"Your mother thought you should learn about my job. You spent Take Your Child to Work Day with her for the past two years." Rob wondered if Logan following him around today could possibly improve their relationship like Mandy expected.

With a sigh, Logan pulled a folded paper from his pocket. He spread it against his leg and flattened the creases. "What's your job?"

"I'm a farrier, third generation." Rob remembered riding with his father when he was about Logan's age and asking dozens of questions. He had followed his father's footprints into the horseshoeing business, like his father before him. However, Rob had married late in life, Mandy didn't want any more kids, and Logan hadn't shown any interest in his profession. The family business would end with Rob.

Logan's pencil hovered over his paper. "How do you spell farrier?"

"It's on the side of the trailer." Rob opened the truck door and stepped out. "Let's go."

"Nichols and Son, Farriers" in bold black letters covered the side of the trailer. After Logan wrote the answer to the first question on his paper, Rob lifted the side door to expose his workspace and tools.

The boy gasped. "What's all this stuff?"

With a chuckle, Rob pulled out his leather apron and fastened it around his waist. "These are the things I use when shoeing or trimming a horse." He pointed out the drill press, grinder, anvil, and forge. Then, he placed the hoof knife in his apron pocket.

A petite, white-haired woman hurried down the barn aisle. "I'm so glad you're here. Bonnie and I went on a trail ride yesterday and now she's limping."

"Let's take a look at her," Rob said. He gestured for Logan to step forward. "Miss Sue, this is Logan. He's learning about horseshoeing today."

The woman smiled at Logan. "You're learning from the best. Your dad always takes such good care of the horses here."

"He's not my dad," Logan said and crossed his arms.

Rob quickly added, "Logan is my stepson."

Sue waved a fly away from her face. "It's nice you're getting to spend the day together."

Rob nodded, but he doubted the day would go well. Logan's tight lips and narrowed eyes reflected the boy's attitude.

They followed the woman halfway down the wide barn aisle to a stall. The wooden nameplate across the front proclaimed "My Bonnie Lass" in bright red letters. A large gray horse poked her head over the stall door and whinnied.

As the woman led the mare out of the stall, Rob watched the horse's hesitant steps. "She's favoring the right front. Logan, see how she lifts her head when she puts that foot down?"

At the boy's puzzled expression, Rob explained, "Horses can't tell us what's wrong, so we watch their body language for clues."

Bending down, Rob lifted the horse's front foot. After examining the sole, he rose and patted the mare's shoulder. Then, he rubbed the stiffness in his lower back. "Looks like a stone bruise."

"Poor dear. It must have happened when we rode over some rocky patches yesterday," Sue said.

"Give her a week of rest, Miss Sue. She should be fine after that. If not, let me know and I'll check for an abscess."

When Bonnie was back in her stall, Rob set to work on the horses scheduled for a trim. From across the barn aisle, he watched Logan approach Bonnie until the horse curled her upper lip.

Logan backed away quickly. "She tried to bite me."

"No, she's smelling that orange you had for breakfast." Rob frowned. The boy's afraid of horses. "Let her smell you."

From under the belly of a bay gelding, he watched Logan inch toward Bonnie and tentatively touch her whiskered muzzle. Good boy, face your fears. "Logan, what other questions you got there?"

With a rustle of paper, Logan read aloud, "What training do you need for your job?"

"I learned from my father, and he learned from his father. I was about your age when I started helping."

Logan came closer. "What did you do?"

Rob laughed at the memory. "I pushed a broom. See all these trimmings on the ground? They'll need to be swept up."

The paper rustled again. "What is your favorite part of the job?"

Slowly, Rob straightened up, stretching his back. "Problem-solving. Yes, definitely problem-solving. Like what we did with Bonnie. You heard how happy Miss Sue was to have an answer to Bonnie's problem."

Logan wrote the answer on his questionnaire. "What's your least favorite part of the job?"

Rob inhaled slowly. "You promise not to tell your mom?"

The boy's eyes widened, and he stepped nearer.

"This has got to be our secret." Rob waited for Logan to nod. "Getting kicked by a horse. It doesn't happen often, but it does happen. I don't want your mom worrying. You understand?"

Logan smiled. "She does worry about things."

It was the first smile Rob had gotten from the boy. "Maybe you should write that my least favorite part is getting dirty. She'll agree with that too." He held his filthy, calloused hands open for Logan to see. "Wait till you see how dirty you are at the end of the day."

They both laughed. Rob slapped the gelding on the rump, and a cloud of dust swirled into the air.

Two horses later, Rob put his rasp back in the trailer and took his apron off.

A slight breeze ruffled the paper in Logan's hand. "Last question. What career advice would you give me?"

Rob rubbed his hands against his jeans and thought about all the wisdom his father had shared. "Be the best you can be at whatever you decide to do."

Logan scribbled the words onto his paper. "All done."

"Not exactly," Rob said. "There's a broom on the trailer. You can sweep up." He pointed at the hoof trimmings on the ground.

For a minute, the two faced each other. Their eyes locked together.

Logan folded his paper and put it in his pocket. "Does this mean you're going to teach me to be a farrier?"

Rob's heart beat faster. "If you want to learn, I'll teach you." Maybe Nichols and Son would continue; another generation might follow in the farrier's footprints.

Originally published in *Footprints*, Florida Writers Association Collection 13, 2021.

The Story Behind the Story for "Farrier's Footprints"

My first year as a member of the Florida Writers Association (FWA) was 2019. Every year, FWA produces an annual collection of stories and poetry by members. In 2021, I decided to submit a short story for the collection. The theme that year was "Footprints" and limited to sixty entries.

The story idea for "Farrier's Footprints" came from my experiences with the Great American Teach-In and Bring Your Child to Work Day. I also leaned into my time with my horses, specifically with the farrier who trims my horse's hooves. While he worked on my horses, I quizzed him on many aspects of his job. Some of his answers are included in the story.

As a newer FWA member, I was thrilled when my short story was selected for the collection.

A New Game
for Travis

Mrs. Helen Willis sat across from the child psychologist, holding back her tears. "Travis still doesn't show any emotion."

"Your son's autism diagnosis indicates level one severity," the psychologist said, reading from his computer screen. "Is he performing basic tasks at home without instruction?"

"Yes, but he's becoming more withdrawn," she said. Fearing a lonely, desperate future for him, she added, "My main concern is that he doesn't have any friends."

After a few more clicks on the keyboard, he locked eyes with her. "What does he do with his free time?"

"He watches one particular Star Trek episode over and over." She rubbed her forehead, thinking of the daily drone of the dialogue. She could repeat every word in the scene.

His fingers glided over the keyboard as he typed an entry. "Which one?"

"It's called 'Where No Man Has Gone Before.' He replays the part where Captain Kirk and Spock play a multi-level game that sort of looks like chess."

"Chess?" The psychologist raised an eyebrow and glanced at the digital clock on his desk. "Perhaps he would enjoy playing checkers."

The next day, Helen enrolled her ten-year-old son in the library's game club for kids. A week later, Travis sat across from a boy named Mason, a checkerboard between them. While the other parents browsed the library's book collection, Helen sat in the quiet game room in case the stress of competitive games triggered Travis. She studied her son's face. It was blank, void of excitement, interest, or nervousness.

"Checkers or chess?" Mason asked, pointing at a box of assorted plastic pieces.

As Travis lifted a black horse-head figure, Helen placed her hand over her mouth. *Chess! He should play checkers. He doesn't know anything about chess.*

After collecting the white figures, Mason placed them on the board. "I go first."

Travis mirrored the placement of his pieces, then leaned forward, his eyes fixed on the board. She was impressed by how quickly he had positioned the various shaped chessmen.

"Chess is fun, but hard," Mason said.

Miss Patterson, the librarian, walked around the room as game time began. She paused by the table and asked both boys, "Have you played chess before?"

Mason grinned. "Of course."

Travis shook his head without lifting his eyes from the board.

"Let me review the moves each piece can make," she said, showing how the various figures changed position and explained ranks and files.

Travis remained silent, his eyes never moving from the board.

Helen hoped her son could remember the different movements. As she watched, the two boys began their game.

Several moves later, Mason scratched his head. "Are you sure you haven't played before?"

Without hesitation, Travis moved his queen. The other boy frowned.

From where she sat, Helen observed the corners of Travis's mouth curl upward in a slight grin. She didn't understand the intricacies of chess, but the body language of both boys suggested that Travis was winning.

A few minutes later, Mason sighed. "You're supposed to say checkmate."

"Checkmate," Travis whispered.

Her eyes stung, and she fought back a tear that threatened to roll down her cheek. Travis hardly spoke to anyone, and here he was talking to a boy he didn't know.

Mason shrugged and knocked his king over. "Wow. You sure did that fast."

At the end of the session, Miss Patterson circulated through the room and spoke to Helen. "If your son is interested in chess, we have two members of the local chess club coming next week to demonstrate a more advanced version of chess. You are both invited to attend. The details are on a flyer by the door."

"Thanks," she said. "But my son never played chess before. He may not be ready for an advanced version. If he's interested, we'll be here."

Driving home, she glanced in the rear-view mirror and saw Travis's hands moving, as though he were shifting invisible game pieces in the air. *Is he replaying the game?* she wondered.

A week later, Helen and Travis entered the library game room. Two gray-haired men sat at a table with three glass chessboards stacked one above another. Travis tugged on her arm. She looked down and saw his wide eyes. A grin lit up his face as he pointed to the tri-level boards. His excitement thrilled her.

Miss Patterson motioned for everyone to take a seat. "We're delighted to welcome two chess masters, Mr. Brad Lawson and Mr. Cliff Jergen, from the community chess club. They'll show us how tri-dimensional chess is played."

Brad Lawson stood up slowly. "Thank you for that kind introduction, but you can just call us Brad and Cliff," he said, then gestured toward the game board. "Chess is a game of strategy between two players. A chess board has sixty-four squares arranged in ranks and files. Each player has sixteen pieces. Today, we are going to show you a more advanced type of chess called 3D chess. Cliff and I love playing this game."

The two men began the game and explained each of their moves. "All the pieces can move up or down levels, except the pawns," Cliff said.

Helen frowned. The squares all had names, and the players kept repeating the combination of letters and numbers for each square as they moved around the board. Keeping track of their moves was making her head hurt. But when she looked at Travis, his eyes were fixed on the three stacked boards. His body tilted forward.

After fifteen minutes, the two men nodded at each other, and Cliff rose. "We're going to stop playing and reset the board. We'd like to have someone volunteer to play Brad. I'll coach you, so don't worry about all the rules. Who would like to try 3D chess?"

Before she could stop him, Travis jumped up and ran to the empty seat across from Brad. She blinked in surprise.

"Looks like we have our volunteer," Cliff said, standing beside Travis.

The audience clapped. Helen took a deep breath and prayed her son wouldn't have a meltdown. Studying Travis's smiling face, she felt a warm glow inside, crossed her fingers, and relaxed.

The chess pieces were set up, and although Cliff leaned close to Travis and pointed to where each piece went, Travis seemed to manage with limited guidance.

Move after move, pawns, bishops, rooks, and queens rapidly advanced across, up, and down the boards. The line of captured pieces next to Travis's side of the board grew.

She noticed Brad and Cliff exchanging glances. Their eyes shone with interest and awe. Her son's gaze never left the boards.

Suddenly, Travis said in a clear voice, "Have I ever mentioned you play a very irritating game of chess, Mr. Spock?"

With a chuckle, Brad replied, "Irritating? Ah yes, one of your earth emotions." He winked at Travis.

Startled, Helen recognized the dialogue from her son's favorite Star Trek episode.

Travis and Cliff were still playing when the librarian stepped forward. "I'm afraid our time is up for today. I hope you liked this demonstration."

"We enjoyed being here," Brad said, while Cliff nodded in agreement.

Helen went to Travis's side and thanked the chess masters. Her hand rested lightly on her son's shoulder.

"You should be proud of him," Brad said. "His spatial understanding is impressive for one so young."

Cliff gave Travis a high five. "You, young man, are a natural. We would love to have you join our chess club as a junior member."

Surprised at the offer, Helen swallowed hard, then gestured for Cliff to step aside with her.

"My son isn't..." She searched for the right word. "He isn't comfortable in certain situations."

"Our club is full of unique individuals. A love of chess unites us. He would fit right in. He has a gift for strategy, an innate understanding of how the pieces support each other, and a rather unshakeable focus. We're chess players, we thrive on challenges."

Helen glanced at Travis, who continued to play the game with Brad. She smiled and beamed with pride at the new direction Travis's life had just taken. "I believe he would like that," she said happily, adding, "and so would I."

Originally published in *New Directions/New Dimensions*, Florida Writers Association Collection 17. 2025.

The Story Behind the Story for "A New Game for Travis"

The theme for the 2025 Florida Writers Association annual collection was New Directions/New Dimensions. My thoughts immediately turned to science fiction and time travel, but I wanted to write something different. I began thinking about tri-dimensional chess, but I didn't know anything about the game.

Several members of my local writers' group, Citrus Writers of Florida, shared their experiences playing 3D chess. I read *The Queen's Gambit*, watched *Searching for Bobby Fischer*, and researched chess and autism. I also viewed several clips from Star Trek episodes and spoke to a mother with an autistic child. Armed with this information, I wrote the story.

"A New Game for Travis" was one of forty-two entries chosen for *New Directions/New Dimensions*.

The Magic
of
Christmas

Grandma's Christmas Cookies

Sitting at her kitchen table, Vickie flipped the calendar page and studied the photograph for December—a plate of sugar cookies and a mug of hot chocolate set on a fireplace hearth. The picture reminded her of making cookies with her mother. Every year, they had spent hours together making Grandma's Christmas Cookies.

The memory of the light, flaky pastry dusted with confectionary sugar made her mouth water and sent her to the pantry, looking for the little box of handwritten recipe cards she had inherited from her late mother. Vickie flipped through the cards until she found the most worn one in the collection.

Removing the card, Vickie smiled at her mother's neatly printed handwriting. The words "Grandma's Christmas Cookies" were written in large letters across the top of the card. Splatters from past use stained the paper and made some ingredients and measurements illegible. On the back of the card, she recognized her childish handwriting from long ago. She struggled to read her words and decided it must be "Angel Wings."

Determined to recreate the tasty cookies, Vickie scanned the ingredients and deciphered the faded letters as best she could. One item at a time, she listed what she needed.

"Flour, eggs, salt, butter. I have all of those." She squinted at two especially stained lines. "That must be powdered sugar, but I'm not sure what this other thing is."

Vickie reached for her phone and called her older sister. "Pam, do you remember those cookies we made with Mom every December?"

"Sure. Those were the ones with the strange Polish name. We always called them—"

Vickie interrupted her. "Grandma's Christmas Cookies."

"Or Angel Wings," Pam added.

They laughed together. Then Vickie asked, "Do you remember the ingredients?"

"How would I know? You got all Mom's recipe cards."

"I have the card," Vickie said, "but I can't make out one of the words. It looks like it ends with the letters UM."

Pam was silent for a few minutes. "Maybe Mom added rum. I kind of remember her giggling when she added a spoonful of something brown. She always said, 'One for the bowl and one for the cook.' Maybe that's why she was in such a good mood."

Vickie studied the worn card. "That could be it."

"Why don't you search online for the recipe?" Pam suggested.

"I hadn't thought of that. I'll give it a try."

As soon as Vickie ended the call, she typed "Polish cookie" and "Angel Wings" into the search box. "Chrusciki" appeared on the screen with a picture of the pastry Vickie remembered. Seeing the word brought back stories her mom had shared about her Polish mother.

Blinking back tears at the thought of her late mother, Vickie scrolled through the various recipes listed online. Some included sour cream, vanilla, brandy, or whiskey. Her mother had never used any of those items in her cookies.

The only ingredient listed on the card that Vickie did not have in her kitchen was the rum. So, she headed to the liquor store. She located the bottles of rum on the shelf and was shocked at the price. "I only need a tablespoon for a recipe," she told the clerk.

He pulled a tiny bottle from behind the check-out counter. "You want a single size like they have on airplanes."

"That'll work!" Vickie left, clutching the tiny bottle.

After returning from the liquor store, she gathered all the ingredients and made her first batch of dough. She kneaded and rolled it flat. With fond memories of her mother, she cut the dough into strips the way she had done so many times in the past. Her fingers wove the strips into the final shape. She dropped the pieces into the hot oil and waited for them to turn golden brown. It took much longer than in the past. When she removed them from the pan, they didn't look like she remembered. They were fat and soggy.

Disappointed, she called Pam again. "What did I do wrong? They're awful and it took forever to cook them."

Her sister laughed. "You didn't roll the dough thin enough. Our arms ached from using the rolling pin over and over again."

"I forgot about that. We used to complain about how much work it was."

"But they tasted so good," Pam said.

Vickie agreed. "They melted in my mouth. I couldn't stop eating them."

"You're making me hungry. I need to eat something sweet now."

"Wait," Vickie said urgently. "Why did they take so long to cook?"

"You probably forgot how hot the oil needs to be. If the temperature wasn't high enough, you cooked them longer, which is why they got soggy."

Vickie rolled her eyes. "I'll have to try making them again."

Her second batch turned out much better. She rolled the dough until it was paper thin and heated the oil to a higher temperature. After the cookies cooled, she dusted them with powdered sugar. Eagerly, she bit into one of the sweet treats. She closed her eyes and savored the taste. It was as good as she remembered.

The cookies were so popular with her family and friends that she made many more batches during the entire month of December. Everyone wanted her recipe. She carefully rewrote the recipe from the card and gladly shared it with everyone who wanted it. Even though she learned the cookie's Polish name, Vickie always called them Grandma's Christmas Cookies.

Originally published in *Peddler's Post*, Citrus County December edition, 2023.

RECIPE FOR GRANDMA'S CHRISTMAS COOKIES

(Chrusciki or Angel Wings)

Ingredients:

4 egg yolks

1 whole egg

½ teaspoon salt

¾ cup powdered sugar

½ cup butter, melted

1 tablespoon rum

2 cups flour

Directions:

Beat eggs until thick. Add sugar, salt, rum, and butter. Continue beating.

Fold in flour and knead until silky.

Roll dough very thin.

Cut into 2-inch x 4-inch strips.

Cut a slit in the center of the strip and turn one end through the slit.

Fry in deep, hot fat until golden brown.

Drain on paper towels.

Dust with powdered sugar.

The Story Behind the Story for "Grandma's Christmas Cookies"

Peddler's Post is a monthly community paper. Members of my local writers' group were invited to write a piece for the publication. I selected December, one of my favorite months, for my submission. When originally published in December 2023, the title was "Grandma's December Cookies."

This story is the most personal piece I've ever written. I have an index card with a handwritten cookie recipe from my late Polish mother-in-law. At the top of the card are the words chruscik and angel wings. She gave me the recipe because I ate so many of her light, crispy cookies covered with powdered sugar.

I tried making the cookies after a church acquaintance gave me her recipe for the same cookies. The two recipes were nearly identical, except one called for rum and the other for rum extract. I called my sister-in-law to verify which to use. Based on her answer, I headed to a liquor store to purchase a bottle of rum. I needed one tablespoon, but all I saw were big bottles. Fortunately, the store employee recommended a tiny bottle like the airlines carry on flights.

The story recounts many of my surprises when making the Polish cookies. My results tasted nothing like my mother-in-law's tasty treats. I haven't tried making them again but might give it another try.

A Donut Dolly Christmas

Behind the battle lines in France, Bridget Murphy closed her eyes, struggling to control the tears that threatened to escape. The green American Red Cross bus, where she and two other women served donuts and coffee to the soldiers, was her safe place. Surrounded by the mixer and fryer, she spent her days smiling and chatting with the young men who came to the takeout window for a hot cup of coffee and a freshly made donut.

Except today, she was more homesick than usual. This would be her first Christmas away from her family. Her lips quivered, and tears streamed down her cheeks. She wanted to be brave, but soon she was sobbing.

Molly stopped cleaning the empty donut baskets and frowned. "Bridget Murphy, stop crying. A Donut Dolly is here to cheer up the troops. Never let them see you cry."

Bridget brushed the tears from her face and sniffled. "I can't help it. Being away from home at Christmas is hard."

"Your eyes are going to be red and puffy," Molly said. "The soldiers want to see your smiling Irish eyes when they come to the window tomorrow morning."

She gave a weak chuckle. "My father used to sing that song to me."

Molly sang with an Irish brogue. "When Irish eyes are smilin'..."

Bridget joined in. "All the world seems bright and gay." Then she paused and sighed. "Only during a war, it doesn't feel that way."

"Listen, girl. Tomorrow is Christmas, and we owe it to those young men who are fighting for our country to smile and give them donuts and coffee. You volunteered with the American Red Cross for this. Right?"

Bridget nodded slowly. Volunteering had been a big decision—her way of being part of the war effort.

"You graduated from college?"

"Yes," Bridget said with pride. "The first one in my family."

Molly stacked the clean donut baskets next to the fryer. "And you're twenty-five?"

"Of course. Or else I wouldn't be here."

"Right. Only one in six applicants qualifies to be a Donut Dolly. You should be proud of that."

Bridget stared at her. "I am. But both you and Lily got Christmas presents from home. I didn't even get a letter."

Patiently, Molly patted her on the arm. "I'm sure your family's package will arrive soon."

"You think so?" The spark of hope brightened.

With a cheerful smile, Molly said, "Sure. Now, let's add some holiday cheer to this green bus."

Thinking of home, Bridget recalled the festive decorations her family had made. "I can make snowflakes by folding and cutting paper."

Molly tapped her finger against her lips. "And we can play Christmas music on the loudspeakers."

"I have a bright red bandana I can wear." She was already feeling better.

"Perfect! That's the spirit."

Together, they decorated the green bus with handmade paper chains and snowflakes. They closed the bus down for the evening and returned to their assigned rooms.

In the morning, Bridget hurried to the bus to start their routine of mixing dough for the doughnuts and brewing coffee. She spun around when the bus' back door opened, and a gust of freezing air invaded the kitchen on wheels.

"Merry Christmas, Bridget," Molly said, closing the door after she entered. "Lily's sick, so it's only the two of us today."

"Good thing I started early." The oil in the fryer sizzled, and the coffee aroma filled the bus.

"Thanks. Busy day to be down one person. Are *you* ready?" Molly scrutinized her.

"I'm done feeling sorry for myself." Bridget adjusted the red bandana tied around her brunette pin curl waves. Then, brushed some flour off her Red Cross uniform.

"Great. Then, we're open for Christmas," Molly said.

"We can do it." Bridget opened the takeout window and greeted the men gathered outside the bus. "Merry Christmas, soldiers."

The crowd cheered and whistled. Shouts of "Merry Christmas" rose among the men. They stomped their feet against the snow-covered ground.

"Who wants coffee and a donut?" Bridget asked.

"I do, ma'am," a fresh-faced private said. His breath escaped in a misty cloud.

She filled a mug with steaming coffee and handed it to him, along with a donut. "Here you go, private. Merry Christmas!"

"Thanks, ma'am. This feels a little bit like home. Those paper snowflakes are just like the ones my kid sister makes."

Bridget grinned. "It's so nice of you to say that."

"My sarge needs a donut, too." The soldier pointed to a dark-eyed man in a stained combat field jacket.

The older soldier stepped forward and pushed back his helmet. "Not yet, Ford. Not until the rest of the squad gets theirs."

Molly joined Bridget at the window. "I have donuts and coffee for the next person."

Bridget locked eyes with the sergeant, admiring the intensity of his brown eyes. "Molly will take care of your men. I can get you a fresh donut and hot coffee."

"I'd like that."

His fast-paced voice reminded Bridget of bustling New York. She found her hand shaking slightly as she handed him the mug. "Merry Christmas."

He took a bite of the donut. "Hey, this is pretty good. Almost as good as my mom's."

"Your mom's a baker?" She leaned through the takeout window to get closer to him.

"Yeah, little bakery in the Bronx."

Her thoughts flew to the little corner bakery her family often visited. "The one on Pelham Parkway?"

"Yeah." He tasted his coffee and finished the donut.

"Gosh, Sarge," Private Ford said. "That's why you're always getting cookies."

"And fruitcake for Christmas," the sergeant added.

Bridget smiled at the amiable camaraderie between the men. "I'm from the Bronx too. We buy hard rolls from that bakery."

"Try the cannoli. It's my mom's specialty."

"I'll write to my family and ask them to buy some."

The sergeant handed the empty mug back to Bridget. "When we get back home, we can go to the Bronx Zoo together."

"I'd like that." Her cheeks warmed and her heart rate increased.

"Bridget, we're almost out of donuts," Molly said.

"Sorry, Sergeant," Bridget said. "I need to go make more."

"Can I help? Despite what mom says, she did manage to teach me a thing or two at the bakery."

"We are short-handed," Bridget said. "I don't know your name."

"Tony Bendetti."

"I'm Bridget Murphy. Come inside the bus." She gestured for him to enter at the bus' back door.

Once he joined her inside the bus, Tony removed his helmet, exposing thick, dark hair. He surveyed the cooking area. "Efficient set-up."

She led him to the fryer. "We make donuts over here."

From the bus window, Molly shouted, "Hurry! I'm on my last dozen."

"Tony, open that bag of dry ingredients." She pointed at the large sack next to the mixer.

"Yes, sir." He saluted sharply, then smiled with a mischievous glint in his eyes.

Her heart fluttered at his playful expression. "Bet you never expected to spend Christmas making donuts."

"I never expected to be spending it with a pretty woman."

She blinked and laughed, while her cheeks grew warm. "Flattery will get you more donuts."

"You have flour on your cute, upturned nose. Let me get it." His fingers stroked the end of her nose. His gaze shifted from her nose to her eyes. "You have beautiful blue eyes."

Her pulse raced. "Irish eyes."

A deep, rhythmic rumble grew louder and closer. She held her breath, recognizing the sound of approaching aircraft. Her eyes widened in fear, and she trembled.

Tony reached over to steady her, taking her in his arms. Listening, he cocked his head. "Ours. Don't worry."

"You're certain?" Her voice quivered. Pressed against his chest, she felt the vibration of his laughter.

"Yeah. Good old American engines. When your life depends on it, you learn to tell the difference."

Safe in his arms, she relaxed.

"Hey. There's a Private Ford here looking for his sergeant," Molly called over her shoulder.

Releasing her, Tony went to the window and asked, "What is it?"

"Sarge, the captain wants you for a briefing."

"On my way." Tony picked up his helmet and turned to Bridget. "I want to see you again."

I want to see you, too. "We'll be setting up in another area this afternoon."

"This war can't go on forever. When it's over, come to my mom's bakery. I'll be there."

"Maybe we can spend next Christmas together," Bridget suggested.

He moved closer. "It's a date. Merry Christmas to my favorite Donut Dolly."

She inhaled his scent, a smell of donut dough mingled with rugged earthiness. "Merry Christmas, Tony. Be careful out there." Her chest tightened at the idea of him being hurt or killed.

He wrapped his arms around her, his lips meeting hers. She leaned into his embrace, wanting this moment to last forever. But he had to leave.

She watched him go until he disappeared into the crowd of soldiers milling around the green bus. Her fingers touched her lips, and she closed her eyes.

Molly came up behind her. "Bridget?"

Beaming, she spun around and said in a dreamy voice, "This is the best Christmas ever—until next year."

The Story Behind the Story for "A Donut Dolly Christmas"

On September 30, 2024, I attended a class on how to write a ten-minute play. The goal was to create two plays on the theme of "Christmas Through the Ages" for performance in the Valerie Theatre in Inverness, Florida. Each student was assigned two specific timeframes. Mine were the first Christmas and Christmas during World War II.

My first thoughts about Christmas during the war went to the battlefield, but I didn't want to write a traditional military story. Doing some online research, I soon learned about the American Red Cross program called the Donut Dollies. The women who volunteered to serve coffee and donuts to military personnel sometimes near combat zones didn't like being called Donut Dollies, but the name stuck.

I read a novel called *Good Night, Irene* by Luis Alberto Urrea, whose mother was a Donut Dolly. My husband told me he had met a Donut Dolly during his time in Vietnam. Soon I was hooked on the idea that my Christmas play would feature these amazing women.

My mother grew up in the Bronx and had shared her memories of life on the home front during the war years. I tapped into her accounts to add those elements to the story.

The play was performed in December 2024 at the Valerie Theatre, and the performers did a great job. The version included here has been changed to add more narrative details.

No Room at
the Inn

HANNAH GAZED OUT THE window of the stone inn on the out-
skirts of tiny Bethlehem. The last glow of sunset was gone, and
the sky darkened quickly. The air grew cooler, and she pulled the
wool shawl tighter around her shoulders. Her husband, Ezra the
Innkeeper, would return soon after feeding the animals in the stable.

She turned back toward the interior, proud of the cleanliness
of the rough wooden table and bench, the bucket full of water,
collection of baskets, and well-stocked storage chest in the far corner. Her endless work kept the place well-tended. *Fetch the water.*
Prepare the food. Wash the clothes. It never ends. No wonder I'm tired.
She returned to the table and lit an oil lamp, then picked up her
mending.

The Roman emperor's census had caused so many people trekking
to the family's birthplace to register. The inn was full of weary travelers
resting from their journey. Their snoring and foul odor filled the

room. Most folks were only passing through. Bethlehem was too small to attract many visitors.

A loud knock at the door interrupted her thoughts. She stopped sewing and put Ezra's tunic back in the basket with the other items needing repairs. "Who can that be?" Slowly, she trudged to the door.

Two men in dusty clothes stood outside. "We're traveling to our hometown and need a place to stay tonight."

Hannah shook her head. "There's no room at the inn. Go somewhere else." She quickly closed the door and returned to sewing. *These travelers keep coming.*

A few minutes later, Ezra strode through the doorway, brushing straw from his robe. "Who was that walking away?"

"More travelers," Hannah said with a sigh.

"Sorry I missed them."

She shook her head. "Ezra, if anyone else comes to the door, tell them there's no room here."

"What kind of innkeeper would I be if I turned people away?"

"One with a tired wife." She lowered her gaze as Ezra studied her more closely.

"You do look exhausted," he said.

"I'm worn out from sleeping on the floor because you filled every bed in the place—including ours—with strangers."

"Not strangers, Hannah. Fellow citizens being obedient to the foolish order of the Roman emperor."

"That may be, but it's okay to say no." She wished he was more attentive to her than to strangers.

"Now, now, wife. We open our inn to those who need a break from their journey."

"I need a break from their traveling, too." She longed for the days before the crazy census, when travelers were fewer.

"You used to be happy to cook for travelers and listen to their gossip and news. It brought you joy."

"I have no joy since the death of our precious little Caleb. I don't understand why God would take him from us." She closed her eyes and lowered her head.

"You know it's not our place to question God's ways," Ezra said.

At a solid knock on the door, Hannah lifted her head and rolled her eyes, while Ezra moved to open it. "Remember, Ezra," Hannah hissed. "There's no room at the inn."

He gave her a crooked grin. "I know." Then he opened the door. "Greetings, traveler."

A stranger with a slightly graying beard stood in the doorway. His robe was dust-covered and thread-bare. He raised his hand in greeting. "Blessings to you and your household."

"Come in. Come in. Shake the dust off your sandals." Ezra stepped out of the man's way.

Hannah moved toward her husband. "Ezra, remember."

The stranger entered the room and glanced around. "I'm looking for a place for me and my wife to spend the night."

Scratching his head, Ezra said, "You seem familiar. Do I know you?"

"My name's—"

Ezra's eyebrows rose in excitement. "Joseph! You're the carpenter's son. We played together as young boys. Your mother always gave us olives and figs."

"Those were fun times," Joseph said.

Ezra nodded, then said solemnly, "Your father—may he rest in peace—helped me build this inn."

"He was a talented man and taught me well." Joseph examined the room. "God has been generous to you, Ezra. You look well. Fine place."

Hannah regarded both men, noting their ease with each other. Then she cleared her throat and nudged her husband.

"Joseph, meet my lovely wife, Hannah." Ezra gestured toward her.

"May God smile on you always. I'm happy to meet you. My wife would be happy to meet you, too."

Ezra slapped Joseph on the back. "You got married! You were always so quiet. I feared you would never speak up enough to find a bride."

"Would you like to meet Mary? She's outside on our donkey."

Ezra chuckled. "Bring her in. Don't leave her waiting in the night air."

Hannah stepped closer to her husband and whispered, "Remember. We're sleeping on the floor tonight."

"Joseph, I wish we could offer you and your wife a place to stay, but there's no room at the inn."

"I need to find a spot for tonight. Mary is with child and her time draws near."

Hannah gasped. "She's about to have a baby, and you have her on a donkey?"

Joseph glanced down at his callused hands. "We had no choice. Ceasar's order must be obeyed."

"We hear that from all the travelers," Ezra said.

"Do you know anyone who might have a little space for us to stay?" Joseph asked. "Just for the night."

"I'm afraid your parents' house went to the stone mason and his large family. So, there won't be any room there." Ezra paused. "Bethlehem isn't much bigger than when you lived here. There's no other inn in town. But—"

"Ezra, remember," Hannah said in a threatening tone. She tapped her foot against the floor.

"We have a stable out back." Ezra waved in the general direction of the stable. "Plenty of room for your donkey. Spread a blanket over the straw for you and Mary.

"Bless you, Ezra." Joseph's lips curved into a broad smile.

"Join us for breakfast tomorrow morning. Hannah is a great cook, and we'd like to meet Mary."

"Thank you, Ezra. Good night, Hannah." With a bow of his head, Joseph left.

Annoyed, Hannah turned to her husband and asked, "Which part of 'no room at the inn' didn't you understand?"

"I didn't offer him a spot at the inn. Only the stable." He gave her a mischievous grin.

"And why did you do that?"

"Joseph and I played together when we were children. He became a carpenter like his father."

"How come I never met him before?" Hannah asked.

"Bethlehem is too small to need two carpenters. Joseph left to find more opportunities." Ezra gave a deep laugh. "And he found a wife!"

Hannah placed her hands on her hips. "What kind of man puts his pregnant wife on a donkey? Imagine being pregnant and riding on a donkey." Then she placed a basket on the table and started filling it with a few items from the storage area.

"I'll leave the imagining to you. I'm tired and ready to go to sleep." Ezra yawned and stretched. "What are you doing over there?"

"Just getting a few things to take out to the stable. They'll need a lamp and some oil. They probably haven't eaten. So, some bread, goat milk, and cheese." She lifted the full basket and headed to the door. "I'll run these things out and be right back."

Hannah closed the door behind her and took the familiar path to the stable.

A few minutes later, she raced into the inn and rummaged in the old storage chest. Trying to be quiet, she pulled out her heavy robe and pawed at the parcels on the bottom. *I know it's here somewhere.*

Ezra's sleepy voice called across the dark room. "What are you doing over there?"

"Mary's having her baby," she whispered. "I'm looking for Caleb's swaddling cloth. It's here somewhere." She kept removing parcels from the storage chest. "Yes! Here it is." She lifted the cloth in triumph and held it to her nose, inhaling the scent. "It still smells like Caleb. I miss my dear baby."

"I do, too. He was such a delightful boy."

Hannah sniffled. "My heart aches for him so much."

"Gone much too young." In the darkened room, Ezra's voice sounded sad.

She fought the tears that threatened to wet her cheeks. *This is not the time for sorrow.* "I better get this to Mary."

"Very thoughtful of you, Hannah. You're a good woman."

With a soft sigh, she appreciated her husband for his remark. "I'm a tired woman. And I haven't been feeling well lately."

"I thought you were mad at me for filling the inn."

"There's that too." *More travelers mean more work for me.* "But I must get back to Mary."

"I'll probably be asleep when you get back. Try to be quiet when you come in."

She stilled the retort she wanted to say. Instead, she clutched the cloth to her chest and hurried back to help Mary.

Hours later, an elated Hannah returned from the stable and kneeled beside her husband, rousing him from sleep. She lifted her lantern toward his face. "Wake up, Ezra."

Turning over, he opened his eyes and shielded them from the light. In a drowsy voice, he said, "Quiet down. You'll wake everyone."

"You must come see," she said in an excited voice.

"See what?" Ezra sat up and rubbed his eyes.

"The baby, a boy. They named him Jesus." She couldn't contain her excitement.

He yawned and laid back down. "I'll see him in the morning."

"No. You must come now. There's a star in the sky. A star unlike any I've seen before. So bright and right overhead. And there are shepherds."

Ezra quickly sat up. "What are shepherds doing here? They should be out in the fields watching over the sheep."

"They say an angel told them to come." Her words tumbled out in an exhilarated rush. "It was hard to understand what they were saying. They are so excited. An angel appeared to them and told them to come see the baby. They're saying it's the Messiah. Can you believe it? The Messiah was born in our stable and sleeps in our manger."

"Take a breath and slow down. You're telling me Joseph's wife had a baby in our stable? With the animals?"

"Yes. And she wrapped him in Caleb's swaddling cloth. My heart nearly stopped at the sight."

"That was kind of you to give them the cloth." Ezra paused, then said in a puzzled voice, "and shepherds were told by an angel to come see the baby? In our stable?

"That's right. They said the sky was full of singing angels."

Ezra struggled to his feet. "And the baby is the Messiah we've been waiting for?"

"Yes." Her heart raced at the thought.

"That's a lot to believe," he said skeptically.

"You must come see for yourself. When you look at the faces of the shepherds, you'll see they believe. And when you look at the baby...."

"What? What am I supposed to see?"

"Mary let me hold her baby, wrapped in Caleb's swaddling cloth. I felt peace settle over me."

"Like when you held Caleb?" Ezra's voice was gentle.

"Different." She cradled her arms across her chest.

"In what way?" A frown clouded Ezra's face.

"When I looked at Jesus' precious face, his eyes were wide open. Unlike any newborn I've ever seen. Then he smiled. A tiny infant. And he smiled at me."

Ezra shrugged. "A happy baby."

"There's more." She stared into her husband's eyes.

"What more?"

Hannah took a deep breath and rested her hand on her belly. "Suddenly, I felt a movement... like a baby moving in me. Do you think it might be?"

His eyes widened. "You think you're pregnant?"

With her face glowing in the lamp light, Hannah smiled. "When I held Jesus and he looked right at me, I knew. It felt just like when I was expecting Caleb."

Looking skyward, Ezra opened his arms and embraced his wife. "The Lord God has blessed us again."

"Come with me," she pleaded. "The night is still. The star is so bright. Talk to the shepherds. Come see Jesus."

He nodded. "Let's go."

"Hurry, Ezra. You must meet Jesus." She tugged at his sleeve.

They rushed to the stable and believed.

Five months later, Ezra and Hannah were blessed with the birth of a daughter. Then, a year later, with a son. They expanded the inn to make room for more travelers and never again said there was no room at the inn.

The Story Behind the Story for "No Room at the Inn"

On September 30, 2024, I attended a class on how to write a ten-minute play. The goal was to create two plays on the theme of "Christmas Through the Ages" for performance in the Valerie Theatre in Inverness, Florida. Each student was assigned two specific time-frames. Mine were the first Christmas and Christmas during World War II.

The idea for "No Room at the Inn" had been passing through my thoughts for years. I always wondered about the Bible story of the innkeeper who turned Joseph and Mary away. What if he knew Joseph from his childhood? How would the innkeeper's wife feel about the situation?

I took those questions and wrote "No Room at the Inn," which was performed in December 2024 at the Valerie Theatre. It was well received by sold-out audiences. Hearing the performers bring my words to life brought tears to my eyes.

A trip to Bethlehem in 2017 gave me a better understanding of the stone structures and environment of the area. It changed my view of what the first Christmas must have been like. The stable was probably a cave, and there was no snow.

The story included here is based on the Valerie Theatre play. It contains the dialogue the actors spoke, plus the narrative that was provided by the narrator, along with added descriptions. My aim was to capture the magic of that first Christmas as experienced by some lesser-known participants.

Acknowledgements

A collection of short stories is only possible because of help from many people and organizations over a long period of time. I want to recognize the groups that created anthologies, since twelve of these stories were originally published by them.

- Florida Writers Association, especially the Collection teams from 2021-2025

- *The Accidental Time Travelers Collective*, especially Josh Bellin and Kiersten Marcil

- Citrus Writers of Florida, especially P. J. Braley, Mary Lu Scholl, and Gary Kenworthy

- *Peddler's Post*, especially Amy Amdahl

- Brooksville Women's Club

Family members have been of assistance in different ways. Two stories in this collection included military history, and Dustin Hill was a great source of information. Joan Bilski created a family account of our grandfather's experience in World War I, which was key to "The Dark Horse."

Individual stories in this collection were reviewed by various individuals over the years. I appreciate all their honest feedback.

Finally, a special thank you to my neighbor and friend, Jean Lindsay, who listened to the idea generation of many of these stories and suggested improvements during our weekly Tea and Talk sessions.

About the Author

K. L. Small lives in Brooksville, FL on a ranch called Carousel Acres with her husband, two horses, four barn cats, and various wildlife. She is a judge for the Royal Palm Literary Awards conducted annually by the Florida Writers Association, and a member of Citrus Writers of Florida. When not writing stories or riding horses, she enjoys drawing and watercolor painting.

To follow K. L. Small's writing activities subscribe to her monthly newsletter at her website: https://kathleenlsmall.com, and follow her at https://www.twitter.com/@KLSmall_Author or https://www.facebook.com/KLSFantasy/.

K. L. Small Books

Women's Fiction

Letters from Shadow Oaks

Short Story Collection

The Dark Horse and Other Stories with a Touch of Magic

Middle Grade Novels

A Dress To Remember: A Fairy Tale

The Brass Ring Series:

The Magic Carousel

The Christmas Carousel

The Haunted Carousel

Coming in 2026

A Carousel for Shade Tree

Bonus: Q & A with Author

Why did you create a collection of short stories?

My initial reaction to the idea of pulling my short fiction together in a book was one of fear—fear that people would perceive the effort as very self-centered. After all, I'm not a New York Times bestseller or celebrity author. However, not every reader wants to sit down with a lengthy book. Short stories offer a chance to take a brief break to escape into a fictional place with a character and reach the end with him or her quickly.

I also realized that with stories that have been published in twelve different anthologies/collections, even my closest family and friends had never read all my stories. So here they are all in one place, plus a few stories that no one has read before.

Why did you select "A Touch of Magic" as the theme for this collection?

Collections and anthologies typically have a theme that connects the entries. Looking at my stories, many of them include some magical elements, whether it's magic buttons, brass rings that enable time travel, a paintbrush made of unicorn hair, or spirits. Not all the stories have magical devices, but there's something whimsical about relationships that work and the wonder of Christmas.

Which story in this collection is your favorite?

That's a tough question for an author. Like parents, we cherish each of our stories. However, my favorite is "The Dark Horse," which is why it earned the top spot in the title and the first story in the collection. As many times as I've read this story, I still get misty-eyed at the end.

Did anything about the stories in this collection surprise you?

The story that surprised me the most when I re-read it in the final review was "A Donut Dolly Christmas." This story was originally written for a stage production done in reader format. That means the performers stood in place and read the script without any movement or props. The play had very few stage directions. I wrote it to highlight the bravery of the women who joined the American Red Cross to provide a bit of home to our overseas troops during World War II.

When I converted it into a short story for this collection, I had to add more details and descriptions, including character actions and emotions. When I read the finished piece, I discovered I had written a romance, my first love story.

How much research is needed to write a short story?

Some stories require detailed research to ensure they are factually correct, even if they are works of fiction. Time travel stories like "The Dark Horse" and "Lake Lorelei" involved learning about things like artillery used in World War I and the policies of the 1920s. Other stories were works of my imagination and didn't entail any research. Sometimes, research means talking to people about their jobs or hobbies.

Why write short stories rather than novels?

As a beginning writer, I was encouraged to focus on short stories. They are a way to learn about creating characters, establishing a setting, building tension, and resolving a problem. The word count limits of short stories teach efficiency in writing. Novels are grand things with thousands of words. Writing a tight 250-word flash fiction piece is much harder.

How can readers provide reviews?

Readers can share their feedback about the complete collection or a specific story by going to sites such as Goodreads and/or Amazon. The review can be as simple as: "I enjoyed (name of the story)."

Why do authors ask readers to provide reviews?

Reader ratings and reactions are helpful, not only to the author, but to other readers. Authors appreciate the time taken to share a sentence or two about how a reader reacted to the book. Excellent reviews are encouraging, but even a low review helps the author understand what might be improved if details are added. Other readers may decide whether to read a book based on the comments in a review.

What else are you writing?

I'm currently editing a contemporary fiction called A Carousel for Shade Tree. It's planned for release in 2026. The story follows five individuals who have experienced a loss. In dealing with their grief, they join in a search for a piece of their small town's history.

Beyond that, I have several Young Adult (YA) fantasies that are planned for release in late 2026 and 2027. One fantasy, Strandlock, won a Royal Palm Literary Award Gold Award for unpublished YA fiction and was second runner-up for unpublished Book of the Year in 2021. I'm excited to share that story and its sequel with readers.

How can readers learn more about your writing activities?

I have a website with additional information about my books and upcoming events. It also contains blog articles that I've created about writing. Readers can subscribe to my monthly newsletter there. The newsletter offers early cover reveals of future books, photos, and bits of information about life on my horse ranch. The website address is https://kathleenlsmall.com.

9 798990 086364